WORLDONFIRE

WORLDONFIRE

MICHAELBROWNSTEIN

OPEN CITY BOOKS

New York

OPEN CITY BOOKS
225 Lafayette Street, Suite 1114
New York, NY 10012
www.opencity.org

Open City Books are published by Open City, Inc., a nonprofit corporation. Donations are tax-deductible to the fullest extent of the law.

Designed by Nick Stone

Manufactured in Canada

10 9 8 7 6 5 4 3 2 1

Library of Congress Control Number: 2001098897
ISBN 1-890447-29-3

Excerpts from this book were previously published in *The Bald Ego* and *Open City.*

The copyright page continues on page 179.

"Grace to be born and live as variously as possible"
—Frank O'Hara, "In Memory of My Feelings"

"Connect me to the world and its people. I am a part of them and they are a part of me."
—Huichol prayer

1.

Panorama of oil rigs, bleached sky, enormous white sun.

Gasoline smell everywhere, you can't avoid it, you can't run inside, there is no inside.

I want to love you, to hold your hand, smell your hair, run my fingers across your brow, lick your skin.

I wish for a lot of things, maybe, but especially these.

Pining for you, unable to sleep in the petrochemical haze, the greasy air, the toxic breeze.

I eat and drink your tantalizing presence nearby, worse in fact than absence.

Because I have you and I don't.

We make love but you're a thousand miles away, your eyes focused on the ceiling.

We make love but you're listening for the phone to ring.

And there is no phone, at least none that works.

It's so preposterous, worse than any joke.

I should have taken it as a warning, I should have known.

I'll never have you to myself.

Your clear glance always denied, averted.

Blood and dust and oil cover everything, the windows, the tables, the chairs.

My lungs—I'm coughing uncontrollably now, my very existence spattered against the grimy panes.

Doubled over, coughing and coughing, stomach sore, I'm frightened, disoriented.

This landscape used to be among the most beautiful on Earth.

Now look at it.

For a moment I can stand up straight again and I breathe deeply.

I look out the window and see huge trucks rumbling by in the sand, each leaking black liquid from behind, trails of crude oil the following trucks slosh through as if during a thunderstorm.

Then—I can hardly believe my eyes—the wells cease pumping, the oil sucked out of the Earth for good, and the endless procession of trucks stops, magically, as if someone's voice which has been calling and calling in vain is suddenly heard.

Will you listen to me? Do you hear me?

Once upon a time—for the longest time, hundreds of thousands of years—the Earth sustained itself.

Forests and meadows and shining lakes.

Herds of animals came and went.

Among them were human beings, communicating in silence with animals, plants, spirits.

Nature was intelligent, it spoke in people's visions and dreams.

Greed—distraction—boredom—cruelty.

You don't believe me when I tell you these things didn't exist then.

Worse than that, you don't care.

It's irrelevant, you say. A fairy tale. A waste of time.

Then why am I chasing you?

Our home is no longer in the great outdoors.

We bivouac in an abandoned cabin, the sagging floors covered with a snowdrift of cold sand, broken tools, shattered glass.

As if everything were inside out, now, once and for all.

I reach out to touch you.

You've aged quickly.

No one would guess this is the same person I followed like someone dying of thirst, up and down busted streets, month after month, and not so long ago, either.

The sun glared at us then.

"I want a new life for us!" I called out.

You kept walking but turned your head to listen to my voice, your hair swinging in the poisoned light, and I was happy.

Now I feel along the cabin walls for the warmth of your face.

Maybe I still need you, maybe I don't.

Whenever we make love now I visualize some unknown wraith from movies or magazines, it's the only way I can get off.

I wonder what will become of us.

Time is not constant, it shakes and folds and twists.

Time is a snake.

The present swallowed by the past.

The future outracing the present.

I hate the way I'm laughed at, ignored, patronized, all because I see the full force of what's coming.

Highways overgrown with trees, oil tankers beached like forgotten toys, the whole petrochemical nightmare vanished.

And in its place?

People are people.

They'll continue to look into each other's eyes and invent the world.

You left me on the morning when the trucks stopped running.

The sky, an eerie lime-magenta mutation, was immense and threatening.

Uncapped fires from the oil rigs blazed in the distance.

I gladly would have killed for you, my darling.

To make me forget you, time gave me a small hand mirror in which I look and see nothing, not even the reflection of my face.

Impossible to say who you are now, who I am.

These days the newspapers are full of stories about genetic engineering.

I want to raise my voice.

"Doesn't anyone remember the last mirage we all took for the inalienable truth of our lives? Doesn't anybody have a snapshot of the cars we rode around in? Isn't there even one shred of diary or memoir to bring us back to those times of noise and pollution and disconnect?"

But instead, I have to tell you, I've discovered someone new—
Jesus, she's so lovely she makes my skin crawl.

I'd gladly have a heart attack and die in her arms this very instant.

She's—but I won't try to describe her.

What could that possibly mean to you?

You who are mesmerized by someone completely different now
too—in fact by the very slob who stands in front of me in line at the
bank, his shoulders slumped, his oily scalp coming apart at the
seams to reveal a tiny frantic brain alive with decay.

Impatient to get to the teller's window and withdraw every last
cent I have in order to blow it on my living dream, for some reason
I turn and look.

There you stand out on the sidewalk, your nose pressed to the
glass, oblivious of everything else, panting for your new beloved.

I wonder if you'll ever even know his name.

In the gathering darkness, none of us able to see.

None of us able to clear our heads and think.

Be still, my heart.

Learn to accept what's coming, sooner than you think.

A new soft-sell eugenics is coming, I'm sorry to say.

People—you'll still call them people.

The question is, what will they call you?

Talk about being shut out.

An ostracism compared to which the schoolyard cruelties of ten
thousand years will seem like a loving embrace.

I'm human too. Don't abandon me.

Flaming trees, melting buildings, air as thick as jelly.

Identical blue faces stacked like cordwood.

Waiting to be selected, waiting to be customized, waiting to be
of service.

The custom job of the near future so brilliant as to be undetectable.

Everyone convinced they're rugged individuals.

Living out their lives on a tasty frontier made of digital pixels and
audio.

While further north the polar ice cap has vanished.

In its place palm trees, giant lizards, disabling ennui.

The Inuit wander disconsolate in the heat, unable to perspire, drowning in sights and sounds of a jungle completely alien to them.

Their disorientation blinds them to the tropical beauty surrounding them.

Lost in the impossible made real.

As for me, I take great pleasure in the color photos I've tacked to my cabin wall.

Photos of car bodies, "modern classics" from the fifties, Malibus and Thunderbirds in mint condition but without tires or even wheels, their axles ground into desert sand.

I admit it, I've always wished for the end of our craven, unworkable civilization, no matter what the cost.

Does this make me a monster?

Compared to whom, though?

Compared to corporate vampires sucking blood from the Earth, single-mindedly reducing all difference to sameness?

Or would you compare me to the para-humans, the virtual millions whose time surely is at hand?

Economic globalization, glorious agenda of sameness.

America's gift to the universe.

Victory of death-in-life.

Cloning is the biological version of this sameness.

It won't work without predictability, control, standardization.

Just as globalization won't work without predictability, control, standardization.

Corporations are legally invulnerable and therefore immortal.

They anticipate the soft-sell eugenics to come.

In fact, they bankroll its creation.

Even before it collapsed, our hallucination was in serious trouble.

But we continued living it, that's for sure.

We loved and fought and played.

We scored and were burned.

We hit the jackpot.

We fell on hard times.

Our bright youth faded.

Our hair turned gray, our eyes grew dim.

Terrible new scourges swept through our bodies.

But meanwhile global capital's trance raged on.

To feed its phantoms the nonwhite world was sucked dry and brought to its knees.

Ecosystems annihilated.

Family lineages morphed into nothing.

Cities metastasized into urban blobs.

People conditioned to disacknowledge the obvious.

In order to understand how this happened, we have to pretend Empire's still alive.

We'll make believe everything's still functioning.

We'll shut our eyes and conjure up Empire triumphant.

We'll pretend the lights are still on, the banks and cafés are still open, the season tickets are still being printed.

We'll have to look at the past as if it's the present.

Not difficult, really.

Since that's the vision which made Empire possible in the first place.

Eaten from inside out, the empty edifice finally crumbles.

But when?

What year is it, anyway?

Centuries ago ancient Mayans predicted world upheaval for the year 2012.

The end of their sacred calendar's five-thousand-year Great Cycle.

Has 2012 come and gone?

The future everyone secretly fears, is it already here?

And the past—did it ever really happen?

The Roman Coliseum, the high walls of the Incas, Easter Island's stone faces, the World Trade Center, all built to last a thousand years—were they nothing more than fever dreams?

When can the monuments of consensus reality be said to exist, no matter how many multitudes have slaved to construct them?

Multitudes in the midst of whose ongoing personal dramas, the actual date remains conjectural.

Since any world described from observation exists relative to the observer.

Perceptions of before and after depending on the perceiver.

Although you're free to watch the evil consummated before your eyes and shudder.

Because now's the time of the motherfuckers.

Whether yesterday, today, or tomorrow.

Whether early or late, inside or out, up or down.

Whether devil or angel.

Which brings us to you, dear reader.

And to me.

The first time I got behind the wheel, what joy!

Sixteen years old, a Jewboy trapped in Bible-Belt fifties Tennessee.

What better way to seek release!

I remember my long slender fingers around the red steering wheel.

Red, red, the Malibu inside and out was blood-red.

My foot to the floor, lost in speed, the original disconnect, king of trances.

How many times, slipping and sliding, have I sped around in circles?

Only recently did I make the connection between human blood and gasoline, the blood of the planet.

You could say I'm a vampire too.

I taste your blood when we make love but you can't taste mine, I won't allow it.

Because I'm a vampire with a conscience.

Hepatitis C.

Who knows how or when I contracted it?

Once upon a time I shot speed with a charismatic poet.

I let him talk me into it.

Or perhaps (how I hate irony!) before traveling abroad in the seventies, those gamma-globulin shots for supposed protection against hepatitis A.

I let the doctors talk me into it.

Is that how I ended up here, by absolving myself of all responsibility?

It's raining now.

The immense desert valley finally softens.

Flames spurting from distant derricks seem to shrink.

They lose their profligate insistence and appear almost playful, spontaneous, innocent.

Then I notice oil wells by the tens of thousands, spread out across the face of the Earth.

Very few of them are softened by rain.

Because even with the shift of the magnetic poles which occurred in the year 2012, even with the extreme changes in climate we've endured, oil and water still don't mix.

Inside my little cabin, water trickles down the walls and disappears in the sand.

Inside my little cabin, mice chew at the thin lilac cashmere sweater you left behind.

Inside my little cabin, the computer screen glows in the dark.

I can't look at it directly for more than a moment.

My eyes ache, my head swells, my heart—anyway, soon the battery will give out, the screen will go blank.

Then if I want to communicate I'll be forced to rely on telepathy.

What goes around comes around.

Those who came before us communicated telepathically, for tens of thousands of years.

Then, for some unknown reason, people lost the ability to sing invisibly.

And now?

Now we depend on wireless mechanisms beaming microwaves into our skulls.

A few short years from now, brain cancer may be the latest—the last—fashion.

Whoever's left will realize that "information" was a strategy of the transnationals, chaining people to computer terminals for the enrichment of a few.

Their limitless greed.

Their boundless egos.

And whoever's left will finally know what the ancients knew:

Communication is experience, never information.

Communication—whirling dervish of the spirit, red glow of the heart—is never about control.

Emptiness, my great friend.

I was right to have embraced you all these years, while others made their fortunes in oil wells.

Or in trading futures.

Or in some other gleaming facet of the grand mirage.

Emptiness, I salute you.

In supermarket lanes and along the crowded concourses of transportational endlessness I stand naked before you.

You've kept me young.

My gaze is fresh and eager.

Even in the city, people stop and stare.

Although these days, I don't go to the city much.

Only true diehards remain.

Everyone else—long ago, it feels like, but maybe just yesterday—everyone else jumped ship.

Because the city's the most vulnerable place of all, now that the end times have begun—services crumbled, unclassified diseases sweeping through the populace.

Not to mention the fact that, without trucks or trains or planes, real food is unobtainable.

Everybody's been reduced to eating gummy bears or spoonfuls of their own stinking shit.

O, to leave the city behind.

To live quietly and autonomously in the sweet countryside, existing on apples and berries and honey.

Or is this just another dream I had last night?

Last night my little cabin barely survived the wind.

It swept along the desert like a razor, carrying with it smells of burning factories, burning automobiles, burning flesh.

I hid my face in my arms and wept.

Asleep or awake, I listened to the wind.

Fallout from the control culture swirled through my brain.

No fewer than four thousand and possibly as many as ninety thousand species dying out annually.

Tropical forests finished at the rate of one percent a year.

Crop genetic diversity vanishing from the field at the rate of two percent a year.

Irrigated soils eroding thirteen times faster than they could be created.

Fresh water consumption twice that of its annual replenishment.

Two percent of the world's languages extinct every year.

Many of the world's ecosystems occupied by people with no indigenous language capable of describing, using, or conserving the diversity that remained.

Cultural diversity being to the human species what biological diversity is to genetic wealth.

The public at large mystified and silent.

How did the end times come about?

Perhaps a short economics lesson is in order.

We'll shut our eyes and conjure up Empire triumphant.

Please forgive the seeming lack of "poetry" in what follows, dear reader.

Please restrain your impulse to tell me you know it all already.

Open your heart, not your switchblade mind.

Think with the blood that those who came before have bequeathed to you.

I'll pick one corner of the mechanism to describe.

Later you can use your imagination to transfer its workings into other dark corners—

Borrowing countries service their international debts by increasing their borrowing.

The more they borrow, the more they depend on borrowing, and the more their attention is focused not on development but on obtaining more loans.

Exactly like heroin.

Exactly like the systems crash diabetics experience.

Integrating domestic economies into the global economy means removing import barriers.

This virus undermines the integrity—the self-definition—of nations.

Increasing the export of natural resources and agricultural commodities drives down prices of export goods in international markets—creating pressure to extract and export even more, simply to maintain earnings.

The very process of borrowing creates indebtedness that gives the World Bank and the IMF power to dictate policy to these nations, whose leaders, in order to stay in power, can only become more and more corrupt.

Diabolique

Foreign loans enable those governments that have bought into the process to increase expenditures without the need to raise taxes—always popular with wealthy decision makers.

This artificial jolt—does it remind you of cocaine, a thousand times more potent than the coca leaf?

Does it remind you of amphetamine?

Does it remind you of petrochemical fertilizers, driving plants to a frenzy of synthetically induced growth?

Parallels everywhere—economic, environmental, psychological, physical.

Drug addiction equals petrochemical addiction equals global capital's addiction.

Nothing is arbitrary, nothing occurs in isolation.

Nothing is left to chance.

Returning to the matter at hand—

Those officials who sign foreign loan agreements tie their people to obligations outside public review or consent.

This becomes especially outrageous when the projects displace the poor, pollute their waters, cut down their forests, and destroy their fisheries.

Then, when the bill comes due, social services and wages are cut to repay the loans.

The bottom line, the arithmetic of need: too much foreign funding prevents real development and breaks down the capability of a people to sustain themselves.

The system works to increase production of more things that people who are already well-off want to buy.

Luxury items for the First World.

Poor people seldom buy imported goods.

Their needs are met by simple locally produced goods.

From the standpoint of transnational corporate capital, people-centered development is a major problem.

It creates little demand for imports.

It creates little demand for foreign loans.

It favors local ownership of assets.

Whereas the "structural adjustment" policy of the World Bank means building dependence on imported technology and experts.

It means encouraging consumer lifestyles, displacing domestic products with imports.

It means recolonization of poor countries by transnational capital.

It means hidden subsidies for petroleum and transport so food from the other side of the planet costs less than local.

It means replacing intrinsic value with utility value.

Diabolique

This arrangement brought darkness to the world, while the sons and daughters of its perpetrators played in DVD fields of fantasyland.

Did these children have any inkling of what their lives cost others?

In Haiti—

"Agribusiness receives ample funding but no resources are made available for peasant agriculture and handicrafts, which provide the income of the overwhelming majority of the population. Foreign-owned assembly plants that employ workers (mostly women) at well below subsistence pay under horrendous working conditions benefit from cheap electricity. But for the Haitian poor—the general population—there can be no subsidies for electricity, fuel, water, or food; these are prohibited by IMF rules on the grounds that they constitute 'price control.' Before the reforms were instituted, local rice production supplied virtually all domestic needs. Thanks to one-sided 'liberalization' it now provides only fifty percent, with predictable effects on the economy. Haiti must 'reform,' eliminating tariffs in accord with the stern principles of economic science—which by some miracle of logic exempted U.S. agribusiness. The natural consequences are understood: a 1995 USAID report observed that the 'export-driven trade and investment policy' will 'relentlessly squeeze the domestic rice farmer,' who will be forced to turn to the more rational pursuit of agroexport for the benefit of U.S. investors. By such methods, the most impoverished country in the hemisphere has been turned into a leading purchaser of U.S.-produced rice, enriching publicly subsidized U.S. enterprises."

(*Profit Over People*, Noam Chomsky)

And what about the science behind agribusiness?

Surely its goal is the welfare of humanity.

Genetically engineered "golden rice" and "golden mustard oil" heralded as miracle cures for vitamin A deficiency, from which millions of children suffer.

Who would reject such a gift?

But look closer, dear reader.

Follow Monsanto's presence in India—

The stage was set by the Green Revolution of decades past.

Instead of millions of farmers breeding thousands of crop varieties to adapt to diverse ecosystems, the Green Revolution reduced agriculture to a few varieties of a few crops.

At the same time, herbicide manufacturers bought up seed companies in order to develop plants that liked their product.

This led to genetic erosion as well as large-scale pollution from agrichemicals.

Mustard greens rich in vitamin A were traditionally eaten by India's rural poor until mustard cultivation was wiped out by monoculture of wheat and one-dimensional breeding of mustard for oil, destroying the edible nature of the plant's leafy part.

Monsanto described its involvement as philanthropic, but breeding was covered by patents, making its rice and mustard the company's exclusive property.

Then, under "free trade" policies, mustard oil was banned in 1998 to allow unrestricted imports of U.S. soy oil.

Imported oil now accounts for fifty percent of India's consumption.

The dumping of oil from Monsanto's genetically engineered soy displacing whatever mustard cultivation remains in India.

And vitamin A deficiency becomes a problem Monsanto offers to solve.

(From "Blind Technology," Vandana Shiva, in *Bija Newsletter*)

●

But how does this lead to the end times, you ask.

How does it relate to drinking the last drop of gasoline?

To an uncontrollable invasion of genetically modified virus?

To losing track of what human means?

Start with the fact that I take advantage of you but I'll never trust you.

You're an eternal threat to me because to enrich myself I have to exploit you.

I put myself in your shoes and feel your resentment.

I build engines of destruction to defend myself against you.

But then I realize it's far better to co-opt you instead.

So I use mass media to neutralize you even before you become a threat.

I'm trading in futures of fear.

I'm projecting my model of the aggressor in every direction.

I don't let up until your uniqueness has been enveloped in my profit machinery.

Until you've been educated to serve me.

Better yet, to join my corporate fantasy which stretches across the seas and around the globe.

In my fantasy everyone sees what I see.

Everyone wants what I want, thinks what I think, eats what I eat.

Everyone enriches my already obscene fortune, enriches it without end.

Everyone serves my insatiable need for more.

Peoples of the wide green Earth, kiss my devious white ass until the end of time.

When is a motherfucker not a motherfucker?

When he's not aware of the consequences of his actions?

But ignorance of the law is no excuse.

Drill her in the heart with your machinery and she'll return the favor with sickness and plague.

Desecrate her fields and she'll suffocate you with pestilence.

Force cannibalism on her cattle and she'll eat holes in your brain.

Ignore her and she'll rob you of your contentment.

Embrace a culture of sameness and she'll hold up a mirror.

And wherever you look, no matter how fast you turn your head, the mirror will remain front and center.

What will you see?

You'll see one size fits all.

You'll see yourself lose your balance.

Once you start falling, how will you stop?

Are you afraid to look in the mirror and find no one there?

Do you scramble to reconstitute the someone who went to bed the night before, ego intact—hell, forget the ego, what about your face?

What about your distinctive body odor, your hard-won achievements, your head stuffed with memories?

You look in the mirror this morning and suddenly nothing's there, although miraculously your usual vantage point remains the same.

The same windows behind you, the same greenery outside.

Yet you're invisible, transparent.

Without baggage, without memories, without a body, even.

And outside those windows behind you, summertime oak trees sigh in the humid wind.

Above them, a prehistoric sky, more green than blue, with clouds so majestic they silence your muttering mind.

How many millions of years have passed and the sky's remained the same?

Before you came here.

Long after you've gone.

History a scrim laid over another order of time—vast, luxuriant, spacious.

History an invention—an insertion—making us believe the only time is clock time.

Clock time doing to original time what enclosure did to the commons, what monoculture does to the forest.

Paradise not a place but a kind of time.

Time in which we once roamed, unbounded and unhurried.

Animals in the wild never hurrying except in crisis.

Unlike our everyday mode of stress, burnout, hormonal loss.

We all sense the cramped artifice, the acceleration.

Everyone knows what's going on but no one will say it.

Chasing the bus of the rest of our lives.

Genuflecting to Our Lady of Perpetual Crisis.

Get 200 anytime minutes, plus 1,000 night and weekend minutes.

A realm of straight lines, of superimposed agendas.

(The first act of the Chinese invaders upon conquering Tibet's wide-open plateau was to assemble forced-labor gangs as an introduction to the State's discipline. These gangs built stone walls in the middle of nowhere, straight lines leading to nothing.)

But the unbounded time of those who came before has never deserted us.

It is primal, everpresent.

It is oceanic, omnidirectional.

Time of the plant realm, almost inconceivably slow for us now.

Almost inaccessible without the aid of an ally.

Without meditation, vision quest, fasting, psychoactive substances.

Something to help break the trance.

I cut the star-shaped cactus into slices and cover the slices with water, simmering them for hours.

During this process their wrenching smell pervades the cabin.

That indescribable aroma.

Its singularity makes me know I'm in the presence of a formidable plant spirit.

Simply cooking the cactus brings that spirit near.

Someone calling from just beyond the threshold of hearing.

Something appearing just beyond the threshold of sight.

Heal me, Momma. Heal me of this disconnect.

I get more and more nervous as the afternoon proceeds.

Many trips to the bathroom. Butterflies in my gut, sweat on my brow.

Anticipation of the psychoactive powerhouse to come.

San Pedro will blow my ego apart, it will leave my identity in tatters.

Glory of the unknown.

Emptiness, my great friend.

An afternoon of preparation has come down to this: half a cup of pale brown liquid which I raise to my lips and drink.

The taste is beyond bitter, impossible to gag down, but I do.

Time passes and my body starts to feel inhabited, tentative.

As if the atmospheric pressure in the entire universe dips and changes.

Suddenly fear gives way to anticipation, acceptance.

I look to rejoin the ancient ones, those who came before.

I look to leave the toxic comic book of consensus reality far behind, my taste for the infinite quenched again at last.

Maybe this time, spirit, you'll answer my question.

Teach me how to survive the collapse which surrounds me in every direction, on every level, at every step.

Make me strong enough to dismantle the demon.

Heal me, Momma. Blow me away.

And spirit tells me this—

"To dismantle the demon, you have to turn and face him.

Because the demon eats your non-awareness.

He drinks your complacency.

Either you turn and face him or he's on your back forever."

Not only face the demon but swallow him whole.

But eating poison's impossible without guidance.

To teachers both human and plant spirit I offer my gratitude.

Their shower of blessings protects and instructs me.

Their gift to me, mind's empty nature.

Their gift to me, fearless presence in the midst of conflagration.

And the demon's solidity becomes my creation.

Evil loses its power, despair no longer seduces.
Faced with the end times I'm renewed, energized.
Empowered by realizations I'd never have otherwise.
I experience hell realms without hesitation.
No more exciting time to be alive than now.

So don't lose heart, dear reader.

Take courage as we enter the dead zone, where planetary decimation is disguised as unprecedented material well-being.

We'll watch, disbelieving, while millions of people are given mysterious new identities.

We'll listen to canned music distract drunken revellers in surfside vacation colonies, while those locals not employed as security stare open-mouthed from the other side of barbed-wire fences.

None of this registering in suburbs back home, where overfed families bicker like strangers, then line up at the multiplex to watch glacial rituals of dismemberment and sexual predation.

We'll swallow all this and more, remaining self-possessed, remaining present, until gradually the demon will shrink, like a tumor in spontaneous remission.

And the space for a new life will appear.

2.

Most of the sites where the U.S. government built nuclear bombs will never be clean enough to allow public access to the land.

They will remain permanently contaminated.

Radiological and other hazardous wastes will pose risks to humans and the environment for tens or even hundreds of thousands of years.

Elimination of unacceptable risks will not be achieved, now or in the foreseeable future.

The government can declare sites off-limits but it lacks the technology to prevent contamination from spreading.

Some contaminants have migrated outside the boundary lines.

Others will follow.

One hundred nine sites around the nation.

Managers may use barbed wire and guards, but it's another thing to maintain such control in perpetuity.

Our governing fantasy, a fantasy of control in perpetuity.

Controls on some of the land already breaking down.

Obviously, no program to minimize the spread of uncontained wastes will suffice over the huge period of time that some contaminants remain dangerous.

Who will be here thousands of years from now?

What will they look like?

How will they think?

Our governing fantasy, a fantasy of control in perpetuity.
Logical, analytical, reductive, judgmental.

If it weren't horrific it would be absurd.

Congress of academic psychologists announcing, "after rigorous objective testing," that people in different cultures think differently.

Any cowherd could tell you if you bothered to ask.

Laughable if it weren't horrific, the tradition of Western "objective" bias.

Slicing and dicing the unknown.

Anthropology reducing native other, biology reducing plant and animal other, psychology reducing cognitive other.

Do you see the connection between "the scientific method" and transnational capitalism?

Arrogant manipulation driving both.

Can you feel the hatred everywhere toward this Euro-American onslaught which has swallowed the world whole in less than three centuries?

Which has reduced creation's splendid array to an arid two-step of cost-benefit analysis?

Timelessly enriching diversity of a tropical forest reduced to the single dimension of a banana plantation.

Self-sufficient, locally driven cultures obliterated in favor of fealty to the global lord, neoliberalism.

Complex social structures replaced by one equation—corporate capital riding herd over an invisible workforce.

Workforce living in wraparound slums in Africa, South America, Mexico, Asia.

Slums growing larger by the day, by the hour.

(Have you visited Bangkok lately? Dare you visualize the Thailand of centuries ago, the thriving villages, open skies, clean water?)

All to provide us with shiny trinkets to hypnotize away our boredom, to slake our overindulged appetites, to feed our cranky, violent fantasies.

You say I'm oversimplifying?

Just look at this.

The split screen never lies—

On the left a photo of a blubbery, testy, arrogant white pig from the northern suburbs leaving a trail of junk-food wrappers, each year generating a mound of trash higher than a dozen villages would have left not a hundred years ago.

On the right a Viking or Celtic or Germanic or Slavic man or woman: fearsome, erect, clear-eyed.

On the left a photo of a blubbery, sullen, precancerous "niggah" of the inner city.

On the right a line drawing of a warrior from a tribe in early nineteenth-century Africa—proud, strong, free.

On the left a photo of a blubbery, pimply, frightened Mexican illegal alien, his innards ravaged by parasites, his mind full of anguish over the poverty of the family he's left behind in order to work in some deep-fried cancer kitchen in a strip mall in the American wasteland.

On the right—

But you get the picture.

Almost always, if we return to the time before the acid wave of colonialism hit tribal realms anywhere on the planet, we witness vibrant health.

We witness true community.

We witness effortless connection to nature.

And that's just the beginning.

Because from the vantage point of sometime this morning, as you've already learned, dear reader, where are we sorry fuckers when the gasoline runs dry?

When the new superrace abandons us as outmoded and out-classed?

When electromagnetic frequencies combine with other question-able vortices to turn our ancient DNA messages into tangled balls of string?

While in the academies, life is reduced to fictional segments copyrighted by the scientific method.

And we insist on treating the plants and animals around us as a backdrop for our delusions of grandeur.

But tell me, what would it feel like to chuck the entire collection of Western cultural baggage?

Have you ever surprised yourself by taking the most monumental crap imaginable?

School's out at last!

Considering what's actually going down on this planet, Western culture resembles Tyrannosaurus rex.

The cowboy brilliance of a thousand white masterpieces, suddenly beside the point.

You sit in your favorite chair trying to concentrate on the latest biography of Proust, on the newest recording of *The Nutcracker Suite*, but it's hard to pay attention with flames licking at the scenery.

Now the curtains catch on fire.

And in that hot light every book becomes another biography of Proust, every performance a version of *The Nutcracker Suite*.

Every prize-winning novel so many novel words.

Every architectural wonder another pile of steel and glass.

Nothing communal, nothing nurturing, nothing empowering.

Better to journey to far-distant mountains and lie down beside a nameless stream.

Listen to songbirds in the branches above you.

Watch the dragonfly on the sapling beside you.

He's hovering there outside of clock time, encouraging you to exhale.

And those wildflowers upstream, their heads nodding in the crystal breeze.

The meadow's covered with them.

They've been waiting patiently for you.

Now they begin to speak.

Shall we go together to the magic place?

To the pure source of all beginnings, to psychoactive wonderland?

Shall we see what happens when ego—surface identity, clutching fear-ridden braggart—is detonated, and the timeless realm shines through?

Light and space, angels of heaven and denizens of the deep?

But maybe we don't deserve that just yet.

To dismantle the demon, you have to turn and face him.

It's time instead for another economics lesson, so please pay attention.

Knock back a double shot of espresso.

Stand under an ice-cold shower.

Whatever it takes to stay awake, to keep a leg up on the competition.

Listen while I sing of the financial sector, as it's so tidily called.

More like a shock wave of sulfuric acid, instantly dissolving boundaries and proportions, leaving nothing but ashen trails of greed.

In the new global market, billions of dollars flow in or out of an economy in seconds.

This forces investment away from production of wealth to the simple extraction of it, de-linking money from value.

Since the end of the gold standard in 1971, the world's currencies have not been linked to anything of value except the shared expectation that others will accept them in exchange for goods and services.

Then came monetary transactions involving electronic transfers between computers.

Money a pure abstraction.

The financial system now functions at a scale dwarfing the productive sector of the global economy.

Twenty to fifty dollars circulating in the economy of pure finance for every dollar circulating in the productive world economy.

Most of the eight hundred billion in U.S. currency traded each day goes for very short-term speculative investments—a few hours to a few weeks.

Money involved in nothing more than making money.

Money enough, each day, to purchase outright the nine largest corporations in Japan.

It goes for options trading, stock speculation, trade in interest rates.

It goes for arbitrage transactions, where an investor buys currencies or bonds at one exchange in hopes of selling it at another exchange simultaneously by using electronics.

Furthermore, the very nature of trading these vast sums is changing.

Financial analysts and traders are being replaced with theoretical mathematicians, "quants," who deal in probability analysis and chaos theory to structure portfolios on the basis of mathematical equations.

Since humans can't make the calculations and decisions fast enough, trading in the world's markets is being done directly by computers, based on abstractions having nothing to do with business itself.

These computers aren't trading stocks, at least in the old sense, because they have no regard for the company issuing the equity.

They aren't trading bonds or currencies or futures.

They're simply trading mathematically precise descriptions of financial products.

The computer doesn't care whether the company makes nuclear bombs, furniture, or medicine.

It doesn't care whether it has plants in North Carolina or Honduras.

Decisions made on the basis of esoteric mathematical formulas with the sole objective of replicating money as pure abstraction.

The global financial system a parasitic predator living off the flesh of its host—the productive economy.

Dear reader, do you see the gaping disconnect between strategic moves and human consequences?

Do you notice militaries of the U.S. and Europe shattering walls of flimsy nations with bullets of depleted uranium?

Obliteration of national boundaries, obliteration of psychological difference.

Vaporization of mystery, death of stillness.

Loss of space, erosion of time.

Claustrophobia, autism, paranoia.

And rage. Rage at being born.

You think I'm exaggerating?

Instead of recounting to me the emerald wonders of the next golf course being excavated inside your gated paradise, trade places with the lives of children in major cities of the world.

Welcome to Bogotá.

Shake hands with a million-plus street kids living in sewers, under bridges.

By eight or nine years of age, many are hardened criminals, addicted to glue and drugs.

Police and middle-class death squads ("hunt clubs") shoot them at night for sport.

Wild, how the parallels just keep coming.

Sick, distorted, out of control on every level.

The twin destroyers of our health—cancer and virus—are not invaders, they're cofactors.

Endless growth, unchecked greed, untouchable etiologies.

And it's not only people who suffer.

Shed a tear for corporations themselves, the final victims of a predatory global economy.

Because corporations prefer a stable and predictable financial climate.

But speculators thrive on volatility.

Just as corporations have de-linked from human interest, finance has de-linked from corporate interest.

Extracting profit from volatility takes many forms.

It's difficult to see how arbitraging electronically linked markets to reduce two-second differentials in price adjustments serves any public purpose.

And futures contracts on interest rates didn't exist until the late 1970s.

Whereas now, outstanding contracts on interest rates total more than half the gross national product of the U.S.

Hostile takeovers decreasing the overall wealth of a society, even as they yield fat returns to the individual.

An investor acquires control of a productive asset or resource—land, timber, even a corporation—and liquidates it for immediate profit.

Split screen again: on the left a Quechua Indian man, chewing coca leaves to give him stamina and reduce hunger as he works in the high mountains. He chews coca leaves for an entire lifetime with no harmful effects.

On the right we see some aggressive kamikaze ghost snorting coke, jumping through fiery hoops of competition, burning out within years—or months.

If the world's central bankers agreed to protect a currency from speculative attack, they could muster at best fourteen billion dollars a day.

Whereas currency speculators trade more than eight hundred billion dollars on a daily basis.

Instability of a global financial system in which hundreds of billions of dollars may move instantly in response to the latest newsbreak.

Perpetual insecurity.

Diabolique

Finally there is managed competition.

Pretend competition, in which the big grow bigger.

Seemingly competing but secretly cooperating with one another to control markets, mindsets, and day-to-day life itself.

Let's take retailing.

A vast consolidation of U.S. retailing has produced giant "power retailers" using sophisticated management, finely tuned selections, and competitive pricing to crowd out weaker players and attract the shopper's dollar.

Telling even the biggest manufacturers what to make, in what colors and sizes, how much to ship, and when.

When Wal-Mart grows at a rate of twenty-five percent in an industry that's growing at four percent, its growth is clearly at the expense of rivals lacking comparable clout.

The mass retailing superpowers—Wal-Mart, Kmart, Toys "R" Us, Home Depot, Circuit City, Dillard's, Target, Costco, you know who—are major players in vast consumer goods networks.

They play suppliers against one another.

They shift their sourcing from domestic to China, Bangladesh, Sri Lanka, Indonesia.

Small manufacturers find themselves in bankruptcy when the major part of their market evaporates.

Only a decade ago, no single toy maker controlled more than five percent of the market.

Now, toy manufacturing is dominated by six companies.

If there's monoculture at the input end (consumption, imaging of reality) there's got to be monoculture at the output end (identity, both cultural and individual).

Sameness.

Corporations are demons, nonpersons given personhood.

Can organizations, like people, go insane?

Is the sanity of a corporation inversely proportional to its size?

Our government—a gigantic corporation in partnership with hundreds of private corporations.

Draw your own conclusion.

The scale of concentration of economic power—

Of the world's hundred largest economies, fifty are corporations.

The world's five hundred largest corporations, which employ only one-twentieth of one percent of the world's population, control twenty-five percent of global economic output.

The top three hundred transnationals own twenty-five percent of the world's productive assets.

In its internal governance structures, the corporation is among the most authoritarian of organizations.

Those who work for corporations spend the better part of their waking hours living under a form of rule that dictates dress, speech, values, behavior, and levels of income.

For all their praise of free-market competition, corporations seek to suppress it at every level.

The argument that globalization increases competition is false.

To the contrary, it strengthens tendencies toward monopolization.

Pretend competition, actual cooperation.

Take the example of agriculture—

Two grain companies control fifty-nine percent of U.S. grain exports.

Three companies slaughter eighty percent of U.S. beef.

One controls seventy percent of the U.S. soup market.

Four control eighty-five percent of the cold-cereal market.

Four mill sixty percent of the flour.

The large firms control the market and dictate how producers operate.

They force farmers to purchase required input from them and buy the resulting crops or animals on whatever terms they choose.

The farmer receives a lower price and the consumer pays a higher price than either would have obtained under conditions of true competition.

This is the system agribusiness is busy extending to the world.

In all sectors, a few corporations strengthen their collective market power through joint ventures and strategic alliances with major rivals.

While broadcasting a mythology of competition in the media and in the speeches that issue from the mouths of politicians.

And producing ever greater profits for its own insatiable master, the global financial system.

"The underlying patterns of . . . economic globalization are persistently in the direction of moving power away from people and communities and concentrating it in giant global institutions that have become detached from the human interest. We have become captives of the tyranny of a rogue system functioning beyond human direction.

"We now face an even more ominous prospect. Having found its

own direction and gained control of the institutions that once served our needs, the system that now holds us captive is finding it has little need for people." (David C. Korten)
Diabolique

Yes, that's a big way the end times came about.

(The hard evidence on pages 19–21 and 33–39 from David C. Korten's indispensable *When Corporations Rule the World.*)

Though the jury's out on what such insights do for us now.

In fact, without a lamp to read by, without a car to drive, without real food to eat, your very existence is probably no more than my own projection.

Still, *somebody*'s reading these lines, I can just feel it.

The sound of labored breathing.

And that mephitic smell from deep inside your gut.

But above all I sense the presence of a mind, temporizing, complaining, belittling.

Because even after Rome burned, the Romans still went on with their lives, didn't they?

After all, what other choice did they have?

3.

I don't know, maybe I've lost you by now, dear reader.

After a hard day's work, who wants to hear about the end times?

In biblical days, the bearer of bad news was stoned into the desert if not beheaded on the spot.

Now you just change the channel.

My frontal assault an insult to humanity, which is either trying to put food on the table or is dressed to the eyebrows and ready to party.

Who do I think I am, anyway?

And in fact that's exactly how you left me, my darling, woman of my dreams, partner of my fantasy future.

It seemed like one minute you were captivated by my rundown of our civilization's venal depravity.

You slumped against the wall in our little shed, your eyes on fire for me.

Gladly you gave your body to me.

Your breasts took me out of this dread realm, all the way to heaven's gate.

And I fell asleep, swooning with your smell, my head against your tummy, my brain finally cooled down, at peace.

Then the next moment.

"The next moment."

Who knows when, really.

It could have been the following morning.

It could have been anytime.

I woke up and it was like another person had climbed into your skin.

Your gentle eyes now hard and mocking.

"I don't know who you are," you said.

I was stunned.

"What are you talking about? We shared a life together in the city, don't you remember? I met your family, got to know your friends."

"We never shared a life together in the city. I only made love to you once, I can't even recall your name. You never met my family or my friends."

From outside the cabin came the groaning of trucks mired in sand, their engines protesting, then finally going dead.

You stood up and tugged at the door until it gave way.

"You think the life I had is finished, but you're wrong. Everything's waiting for me, everything's exactly the way it was. I'm returning to reality now. You can't stop me."

Then you were gone.

I stumbled through the lime and magenta oil-slick haze, eating desert sand, drinking rodent piss, desperate for your succor.

Until, turning the corner around another adamantine boulder, I stopped in my tracks.

There you were.

You could have knocked me over with a chopstick, I was so startled by your transformation.

You'd entered the state of denial with a vengeance, clutching a dead cell phone in one hand and the remains of a rubber-hard burger in the other.

As I approached I could hear the unmistakable mantra of the media gods dribbling from your blistered lips.

A litany of celebrity gossip, corporate logos, fashion styles and fabrics, movie plots, newspaper headlines, political scandals, golf scores, prescription drugs, and especially automobiles—their names, dimensions, interiors, prices.

That's when I knew you'd lost it, because none of that stuff was available anymore.

It had all been sucked into the vacuum, irretrievable.

Yet you'd lost your ability to see this.

You kept thinking it was actual, tangible.

You were now one of the undead, my darling.

Drowning in an acid rain of vanished commodities and still calling out for more.

But isn't there a way to separate your spirit from the rest of you and start over?

Your spirit, luminous and clear, which I glimpsed when we first met.

Spirit which had freely bestowed your unguarded smile on me, the greatest gift of all.

Where was that smile now?

Speaking of chopsticks—

Chopsticks of the Borneo rainforest, now there's a cautionary tale.

Once upon a time a young Canadian woman—Biruté Galdikas by name—came to the forests of Borneo to protect what was left of the primeval orangutan population. And to reclaim the orangutans imprisoned in cages and backyards throughout Indonesia.

In what turned out to be her life's work, with the stubborn dedication of a missionary, she spent decades winning over a corrupt, uncaring government. Befriending, cajoling, browbeating. Until finally a part of the forest was declared a national preserve, off-limits to hunting and forestry. And there she rehabilitated babies whose mothers had been shot down out of the trees, murdered for a trade in pets. She patiently gave them food and space, allowing them to grow used to the wild again.

Then everything changed.

This preserve lay on one side of a jungle river.

On the other, behind a screen of trees which made the area seem untouched, thousands of acres were clear-cut by a Japanese corporation to make chopsticks. And the Japanese wanted her preserve. They didn't give a damn about her work with orangutans. They didn't give a damn about the jungle. They just wanted their chopsticks.

Soon Biruté no longer felt safe. Shots were fired at her as she worked with her orange-haired friends in the forest. She was forced to hire bodyguards. Then her agreement with the government was terminated.

Paranoid, her health deteriorating, before too long she was hustled off the preserve to a nearby town.

Situation pending.

Pitiless story repeated countless times around the globe.

Engine of greed erasing regions, erasing wildlife, erasing communities, forcing generations of newborns into lives as bit players in the new colonialism.

Solidifying the hallucination of our high-tech pleasure garden.

Which doesn't even exist except in the minds of true believers.

Except in the minds of global capital Holy Rollers, corporate fundamentalists.

Ah yes, dear reader. At last you're beginning to acquire some respect for the power of consensus reality.

Talk about a magic trick!

Sucking an entire planet through its sleeve.

Creating nothing where something existed.

But why?

That's the big question.

I asked it the first time I journeyed with ayahuasca.

Vision vine, great teacher, vine of the dead.

I drink the bitter brew, its DMT whiff making me almost puke even before I swallow it.

First the waiting period, thirty or forty minutes during which there's ample time for a desperate parade of second thoughts—why am I here, whatever possessed me to do this, why aren't I safe at home?

Then comes the shift in atmospheric pressure, a subtle alteration at first.

Wait, maybe I'm changing my mind about this.

Maybe I'll just get off here. Ha ha ha!

HA HA HA

Great tsunami.

Tidal wave approaching with such force my body quakes in trepidation.

I'm lying in the dark on a mattress, surrounded by a dozen or so fellow travelers.

I can hear moaning and nervous laughter.

Then I'm on my own.

Uneasy anticipation suddenly gives way to an explosion of visions—breathtaking colors, hypnotic patterns evolving and devolving, bursting without warning into a panoply of gesticulating figures.

Are they people? Cartoon entities? Fairy folk? Demons?

Yes, damn it, they're grimacing, pulsating demons!

Any second now they're going to open their jaws and gobble me up.

Nowhere to run, nowhere to hide.

Disabling fear, paralyzing, suffocating.

But then an extraordinary relationship develops between my emotional state and the antics of these figures—I realize that it's my fear which allows them to become ferocious.

Loss of breath makes them threatening.

As soon as my tension dissolves they erupt in laughter!

This titanic 3-D movie which is invading me from "outside"—if I'm terrified, the demons are inescapable.

But if I'm brave enough to breathe fully and calmly they mutate, becoming puckish, playful, manageable.

Then something further reveals itself.

Several Indians appear, surrounded by light rays spraying out in all directions.

I find myself in silent communion with one man in particular.

As soon as we become aware of each other I'm overwhelmed with sadness at the suffering of the planet.

End times played out in monstrous unconsciousness.

People seemingly in trance as the consequences of their actions burn away everything around them.

Greed, violence, diseased intentions, stupidity, punching holes right through life.

I approach this man in his dusty, tattered poncho.

I don't need words to convey my heartache.

Silently I ask him, "The world's being trashed, destroyed. What can I do?"

He responds by looking straight at me, holding my glance, not letting go.

My mind stops.

He floats toward me, his eyes pulsating, throwing off intense heat.

Hyperventilating, fighting to maintain composure, I begin to panic.

But then I remember to breathe.

I force air through my stiffened lungs, slowly and deeply.

In and out. In and out.

I give up trying to understand.

His eyes fill with compassion.

Their heat turns to warmth, comforting and reassuring me.

I feel safe enough to weep for myself, for everyone I've ever loved and hated, for all of us on this Earth who are slugging it out and can't find our way.

Now he's very close to me, his eyes enormous.

I try to focus on both but can take in only one of them.

I look into its pupil, and in that black space I see a globe turning and turning, rolling through time.

I watch, dumbfounded, as world ages come and go.

Blue, green, white.

Blue, green, white.

Then tiny beads of red appear, their light rich and clear as rubies.

For the longest time they slowly expand.

But as they merge into large, irregular shapes, covering more and more of the Earth's surface, the quality of their color changes to a sickly, grayish orange, dull and greasy.

"O my god," I moan. "Like a plague . . ."

At the very moment I say this, the ball loses all of its color, becoming transparent.

It continues to spin, solid rock crystal.

Empty in essence.

Luminous in nature.

Refracting whatever I project into it.

Ego's fear-based agendas not innate.

Control in perpetuity not innate.

What's been given away can be taken back.

We share the same planet.

We share a common destiny.

As I start to come down, I'm aware of the men and women around me.

My fellow travelers huddled in their blankets, giggling and whispering.

I have such affection for them.

I can't wait to talk to them, to look them in the eye.

I inhale and exhale, feeling an indescribable pride in my physical being.

Outrageous, how right it is to be alive!

I've been flat on my back, legs splayed, for what seems like days, but now I raise my knees and feel the weight of my feet on the ground.

Nothing—no matter how pernicious—will take away that strength, that connection to the Earth.

And now, another question.

Great liana emerging from the jungle floor, how to explain the magical embrace between my chemistry and yours?

Why ayahuasca (and so many more teaching plants) in the Amazon Basin?

Why the relative scarcity of psychoactive substances in the Old World?

Then I remember that in prehistory's global migration, South America was the final destination.

The Amazon basically the end of the line.

And there in the trackless jungle, patiently waiting . . .

So I sense a vast intelligence.
Of which I am a part.
Witnessing in real time Empire's conflagration.
Seeing it, tasting it.
Flinching from nothing, afraid of nothing.
Emerald goddess of the Amazon, heal me.
Mi corazón.

The next morning, sharing our experiences in a circle, we're amazed to discover that at some point during the night everyone saw the globe turning.

Everyone saw the end times hit, everyone understood why.
Consensus reality insubstantial, made of images and beliefs.
The instant we change them, they vanish.
The instant we change them, a new world appears.
Fire meaning purification, cleansing, renewal.
Life renewing itself and our individual selves (our names in the phone book) following—like it or not, ready or not.
We've restricted consciousness to individual egos, but consciousness has no restrictions.
Human brains don't make it.
A larger force is at play.
The view we hold now no longer serves us.
Everything going up in flames, everything purified, renewed.

Global change for the good is inevitable.
Competition actually contained within a larger circle of bonding and cooperation.
The way communities operated before Empire.
And, beyond the reach of Empire, continue to operate.
Global change devouring a doomed test-tube mutant.
Whether early this morning or sometime next week.

Because what if dark didn't always mean evil?

What if the Devil didn't always exist?

Ego cancer a relatively recent distortion, the product of a low-level trance.

A purposive trance, utilized by interested parties for their own gain.

Evil mutated, overpowering good, pulverizing it, blowing it away.

The planet's two hundred richest people doubling their net worth in the four years to 1998.

The assets of the top three billionaires more than the combined gross national product of all least-developed nations and their six hundred million people.

World out of balance.

Anamorphic. Meretricious.

Not since the beginning of time, but since the beginning of history.

The certainty that some are born free and others are born to be slaves has guided empires since history began.

"But it was with the Renaissance and the conquest of the Americas that racism became a system of moral absolution at the service of European gluttony. Since then racism has ruled, dismissing majorities among the colonized and excluding minorities among the colonizers. In the colonial era racism was as essential as gunpowder."

(*Upside Down*, Eduardo Galeano)

Some rough estimates of the action—

In Haiti, the native population reduced from 100,000 to 250 in fifty years.

In Mexico, reduced to one million from twenty-five million after eighty years.

Reduced in Peru from ten million to 1.3 million in a hundred years.

Indigenous peoples of the U.S.A. reduced from five million to 220,000 by the year 1800.

Seven million Amazonian Indians reduced to 900,000.

A total of forty million.

Does that take the grand prize?

World out of balance.

Anamorphic. Meretricious.

Sickness now called health, decay now called youth, resignation now called normalcy, suspicion now called trust, destitution now called plenty, mud slides now called summer, drought now called winter, erosion now called earth, plantations now called forest, GMOs now called plants, virus factories now called animals, androids now called humans, remote control now called democracy, surveillance now called community, fear now called love, clocks now called time, time now called money, money now called freedom, freedom now called work, work now called life.

Arbeit macht frei.

Heal me, Momma.

Heal me from the ornate contortions of human invention.

Heal me from allopathic medicine!

Our greatest achievement?

Hopeless really, because its mode of perception sees nothing but symptoms.

Since causes are not addressed, the situation usually worsens over time.

The only response, more and more ingeniously baroque techno-logical interventions.

The only response, abject reliance on a synthetic pharmacopia.

Wishing the enemy would just go away.

But is there even an enemy out there in the first place?

The completeness of life lost in delusionary reductivism.

Compare allopathy to the clarity and simplicity of worldwide herbal traditions.

Compare it to homeopathy or ayurveda.

Compare it to Tibetan or Chinese medicine—to any system which looks for causes rather than being hypnotized by effects.

Effects—surface—symptoms.

"Go away, evil bastard, betrayer virus, creepy cancer."

But the Devil's not lurking in darkest night.

He's our invention, creation of our rampant toxemia, betrayer of our life blood.

Poisoner of our body's own terrain, where all disease flares up and catches fire, raging uncontrolled, transforming itself into bacteria, yeast, fungus, mold, cancer, virus, AIDS.

Spend your life vainly inventing an armory of protection, one drug more complex than the last, with deeper and more corrosive side effects.

But above all, attack.

Attack is the only answer.

Crush the threat before it has a chance to strike.

See all of creation as fear-inducing threat.

Potential enemies everywhere.

The ornate contortions of human invention . . .

This brings us to a nasty problem: why has the development of civilization resulted in tyranny, cruelty, greed?

Because the advent of agriculture and domesticated animals, the invention of personal wealth, are recent, going back no more than six or eight thousand years.

Before that, for ages beyond reckoning, we wandered the globe, following its curves, its seasons, its secrets.

Hunter-gatherers, as they're labeled, except even this appellation is infected by our product mentality.

Our bottom-line illness.

The key word here is "following."

Our forebears didn't presume to lead. They followed.

They followed herds, appearance of fruits and seeds, flocks of birds, migrations of fish.

They followed constellations in the sky, tracks of animals in the bush, the helping hand extended by plant spirits.

They followed streams, forests, mountains.

They followed clouds, storms, omens.

They followed the dream of life and were connected to it.

And we, who were taught to deride them as primitive, quaint, dull—to what degree can we say we too were connected?

Before our oil wells ran dry, that is.

Before our soil gave out.

Before our water glowed in the dark.

To the contrary, we lived in a fraction realm, understanding next to nothing.

Why did I work year in and year out at a job I detested?

Why did I get more pleasure from fantasies of domination than from the embrace of my own life partner?

How did the computer on which I depended actually function?

The electrical grid without which I couldn't imagine existing, how did it operate? Where did it begin or end?

The pharmaceuticals which only made us sicker, why were we ingesting them?

The EMF radiation that cooked our brains, the chemicals that polluted our waters, where did they come from?

Armaments which blackened the sky, which tore apart nations, turning their children into killers, who took responsibility for them?

How bored we were, when our television sets finally went blank.

Bored and terrified.

And that was just for starters.

O frequent flyer to anywhere tropical, who were those beings on the parched Earth beneath your wings?

How did they pass their time, besides working on absentee-owner factory floors in a sea of bad fluorescent light?

"The punishment of Tantalus is the fate that torments the poor. Condemned to hunger and thirst, they are condemned as well to contemplate the delights dangled before them by advertising. As they crane their necks and reach out, those marvels are snatched away. And if they manage to catch one and hold on tight, they end up in jail or in the cemetery.

"Plastic delights, plastic dreams. In the paradise promised to all and reserved for a few, things are more and more important and people less and less so. The ends have been kidnapped by the means: things buy you, cars drive you, computers program you, television watches you." (Eduardo Galeano)

How could such titanic dysfunction take place?
"Human greed . . ."
An unavoidable explanation, although hardly the whole story.
Because before the stockpiling of harvests, there was no surplus.
No riches and the need to defend them.
There was very little to get greedy about.
Problems existed, certainly, unwelcome surprises.
Enemies over the next hill, natural disasters.
But no betrayal within the clan.
There was no class system, no haves and have-nots, no bosses and slaves.
No divine kings.
There was no priestly mediation between people and the mystery surrounding them.
No temples with their bottomless wealth.
No organized religions with their vengeful, competing dogmas.
No sacred texts to be defended to the death.
No "chosen people."

We need to see how greed works, though.
We need to understand how pitiless it is, how wasteful and stupid, even to the point of self-immolation.
Let's look at the petrochemical game.
(Thanks for what follows to Christopher Bird's and Peter Tompkins' *Secrets of the Soil*.)
The energy industry has known for over fifty years that there's a cleaner, cheaper way to power internal combustion engines than fossil fuel.
For over half a century, an open secret that internal combustion

engines can run solely on alcohol or on gasoline with an alcohol additive.

But you didn't know, did you?

That's because billions of dollars going into somebody's pockets each year depend on your ignorance.

To make auto fuel from fresh plant tissue is economically feasible.

It's as easy as making it from the fossilized remains of plants.

But living plants have an enormous advantage—they're renewable, yearly and indefinitely.

Low-pollution fuel from fresh plants would also reduce the greenhouse effect by cutting down on industrial proliferation of CO_2.

It would create a great mass of vegetation.

Organic wastes from this bonanza would help rebuild a degraded soil.

Alfalfa, producing enough vegetation to yield the energy equivalent of two to seven barrels of oil per acre.

Corn, producing the equivalent of twenty barrels per acre.

The two grown together—intercropped—would erase the need for (petroleum-based) fertilizer, because alfalfa, like most legumes, takes nitrogen from the atmosphere and puts it into the soil.

Other highly fuel-productive plants include rice, sorghum, and the taller grasses.

The fifty-five million tons of protein derivable from sixty-two million acres of land now lying fallow in the U.S. are about ten times what Americans need for their diet.

What remains after protein extraction would yield the yearly equivalent of 250 million barrels of oil in the form of alcohol from cellulose broken down into sugar.

This is just an example of using land not presently farmed.

What would happen if a coherent policy were instituted nationwide?

Before long we'd be looking at the utter obsolescence of petrol.

And since petroleum by-products are the leading source of chemicals and drugs poisoning us and our environment, what we're really looking at is a revolution—taking out the entire petrochemical industry.

Redefining where and how we get our fuel.

And by extension, redefining how and with what we grow our food, how and with what we heal our bodies.

So it's not only the auto-fuel industry which depends on our ignorance.

It's the drug companies, too, and the fertilizer, insecticide, and herbicide producers, many of which are the same transnationals.

Talk about a house of cards.

Huge, monolithic, powerful—but ultimately vulnerable.

No wonder you've never heard about ethyl alcohol's no-brainer feasibility as fuel.

Because actually, grain alcohol's been used since before the Second World War.

In fact, during that war, due to petrol shortages, alcohol was used in America's bomber planes, although Roosevelt could only do so as an emergency measure.

And alcohol is still used for race cars and speedboats.

The technology hardly unproven or experimental.

Fuel converters could easily be manufactured and installed by the automobile industry.

In the United States alone, the 125 million acres presently used to grow hay and corn for livestock could be made into "energy farms."

After harvesting for local consumption and for export of 100 million tons of legume protein, enough biomass would remain to generate 3.5 million barrels of oil.

That would take care of the country's entire energy requirements.

But even without kicking the beef habit, obviously a great deal of our dependence on petrol could be made to vanish.

Farmers could distill their own fuel on their own farms, or make larger amounts in a community distiller—out of any crop containing sugar or starch.

And worldwide, alcohol is also the best alternative because it can be produced within each country, whereas petroleum has to be imported.

So why aren't we using grain alcohol?

As long ago as the 1930s, all this was known.

Books were written, proposals were made.

And the opposition of the oil companies was organized and brutal.

They frightened the public into believing alcohol was inefficient or dangerous.

Money gushed like oil to lobby senators and congressmen.

After alcohol's emergency use during the Second World War, the government closed down its alcohol refineries.

While grain was being stored in bins, elevators, vacant lots, tents, ships, and even on the main streets of towns, each bushel of grain containing better than two and a half gallons of ethyl alcohol, the farmer was subsidized to retire land from use.

Now that cheap gasoline is a distant memory, the petrochemical companies, mindful of the depletion of their oil reserves, are manipulating farmers into debt and expropriation by foreclosure in order to control the source of biomass.

When this process has gone far enough—when the fields and ethanol processing plants are owned by transnationals like ADM— perhaps you'll hear about living sources of energy.

As you've no doubt heard about how tightly petroleum fits into the New World Order.

So many business deals, so many players with powerful government connections.

These players must have known that, by 1998, as much as ninety percent of the planet's crude oil had already been found.

A single month's military budget spent on making alternative energy sources affordable might have changed everything.

Yet they couldn't restrain themselves.

With the global economy overrunning its natural capacities, what did they think would happen as China, India, and other fast-developing countries emulated the American lifestyle?

"If car ownership and oil consumption per person in China were to reach U.S. levels, then China would consume eighty million barrels of oil per day. Yet, in 1996, the entire world produced only sixty-four million barrels per day."

(*Promise Ahead,* Duane Elgin)

"Consumer society is a booby trap. Social injustice is not an error to be corrected, nor is it a defect to be overcome; it is an essential requirement of the system. No natural world is capable of supporting a mall the size of the planet." (Eduardo Galeano)

Greed not restricted to any one color or nationality, obviously.

Third World managerial classes gaily milking their own people, offering transnationals anorexic wages and a disposable environment.

But let's not forget that America's the prime example.

The U.S. (five percent of Earth's population) selling half the weapons in the world and buying one quarter of the oil.

Such junkie economics cushioned by consumption of more than half the sleeping pills, tranquilizers, and other legal drugs sold worldwide, as well as half the illegal drugs.

4.

Of course, all that's ancient history.

The year 2012 has come and gone.

The oil's gone too now.

The land is poisoned, it's as hard as a skillet.

The seeds are neutered, the fertilizer stands in sacks against the wall.

The big machine's been turned off, the plug's been yanked out of its socket.

No matter how many millions still sit in the blue haze of television screens long dead.

Inventing that haze.

Insisting they're "interacting."

Guffawing in their living rooms at literally nothing.

No matter how many debased sensoriums drift in a three-dimensional trance of noise, gadgets, and trash.

No matter how many years still pass in deadly serious game-playing, even after the lights have gone out, even after the scorecards have turned to dust.

But you and I know things are different.

Our asses out on the barren desert floor, we've tasted actuality.

We know the truth.

We know that in these end times, everything's the opposite of what it seems.

"Red-blooded male," for example.

He thinks he gains his power from consuming red meat, so he eats more and more of it.

He bulks up in order to meet the challenge of a hostile universe.

Apparent meaning: his strength and aggressiveness make him impregnable.

Fortress male, dominator of the free world.

Actual meaning: because he also gobbles vast amounts of sugar and starch, because he drinks alcohol, yeast and fungus bore holes in his distended gut.

Over the years, undigested animal protein passes through the holes into his blood stream.

Becoming an agent of toxicity, it destroys red blood cells, making the terrain acidic so that only yeast and fungus can grow.

Yeast and fungus, agents of decay.

Precursors of mold and rot.

End times within, end times without.

O great warrior, unbeknownst to you the enemy's breached the walls and is streaming through your body, replacing light with shadow, substituting death for life, clouding your judgment.

A vicious circle begins to tug at you, pulling you down.

By the age of fifty—if not sooner—red-blooded male has major problems: arthritis, colitis, clogged arteries, diabetes.

The life force he's counted on since he was a teenager seems to have deserted him.

He becomes depressed and full of rage, taking it out on his wife, the kids, his competitors.

Enemies are everywhere now, nefarious and shape-shifting.

His only option to develop ever more extreme ways of dealing with them.

The fear of God in him, he rushes into the embrace of the bumbling and the ignorant—the best and the brightest.

He listens to allopathic physicians whose sole approach is suppression of symptoms.

They lead him into a chemical wasteland from which he can't find his way out.

(Prescription drugs a leading cause of American deaths. Pharmaceutical companies in the U.S. alone spending $1.3 billion a year on advertising.)

Allopathic physicians take him there because they know no better, their training off the mark.

The time and effort they've invested in becoming doctors rarely allowing them a fresh look at their patients.

Most of them refuse to consider time-honored ways of dealing with disease.

Simple ways, gifts of the plant spirits.

In a world full of guile and betrayal, how could healing possibly be simple?

They know only complex products of the laboratory, which at best buy a little time.

Ah, pharmaceuticals—is it any coincidence that many of them are manufactured from petrochemicals?

Or that petrochemicals also furnish the pesticides sprayed on the grain which cattle eat?

Forests of entire nations converted to rangeland to feed the craving for beef.

Which itself slowly enervates the very master race that craves it.

Anti-spiral, anti-vortex, sucking the light out of life.

Diabolique

Amount of total U.S. grain production consumed by livestock: seventy percent.

Amount of U.S. cropland producing livestock feed: sixty-four percent.

Amount of U.S. cropland producing fruits and vegetables: two percent.

Pounds of edible product that can be produced on an acre of prime land: cherries: five thousand; green beans: ten thousand; apples: twenty thousand; carrots: thirty thousand; potatoes: forty thousand; tomatoes: fifty thousand; celery: sixty thousand; beef: 250.

Calories of fossil fuel expended to produce one calorie of protein from beef: seventy-eight.

Calories of fossil fuel expended to produce one calorie of protein from soybeans: two.

Amount of Earth's landmass grazed by livestock: one half.

Amount of world grain harvest consumed by livestock: one half.

Activity that accounts for more than half of all water consumed for all purposes in the U.S.: livestock production.

Amount of waste created by ten-thousand-head feedlot: equal to a city of 110,000 people.

Number of people who could be fed using the land, water, and energy that would be freed up from growing livestock feed if Americans reduced their intake of meat by ten percent: ten million.

Number of children who die as a result of malnutrition and starvation every day: thirty-eight thousand.

(From "Realities for the Nineties," John Robbins, in *Diet for a New America*)

So your average American steer eats twenty-one pounds of plant protein to produce one pound of protein in steak.

Which only ends as putrefaction in the human gut.

Furnishing billions of dollars worth of business for the pharmaceutical industry.

Which in turn owes its existence—remember?—to the oil industry.

Daisy chain, black hole, dizzy spell.

Meat-eating contributes to the fear in the world by reinforcing the notion that there's not enough to go around.

Of course, if America took the unpalatable step of adopting a vegetarian diet, all that grain could be saved for energy production.

But how would our red-blooded male meet the challenge of a hostile universe if he stopped bulking up on tainted meat?

(The two go together. Hostile universe, tainted food. No doubt his world would be different if he ate wild, uncorrupted animal flesh. But he can't, because the vision which constitutes his life is rotten. It seethes with fungus and mold. In order to maintain it, he needs decaying flesh, hundreds of pounds each year. He commandeers forests and meadows, turning them into pastureland. He injects his cattle with antibiotics so they'll survive the conditions under which they're raised. He kills them in torture chambers, no better than concentration camps, rife with disease and suffering. His disconnect so extreme that all he allows himself to see of this process is shrink-wrapped packages of bright pink flesh on supermarket shelves. His breath stinks, his hands tremble, he grows corpulent and radiates a vile toxicity. He and his kind generate more unusable waste than a nuclear weapons site.)

But he won't survive for long, even if he still exists, that is.

Which—except as a feedback mechanism corroborating his own projections—he doesn't.

Although he's convinced he's firmly in control.

Because when fantasy becomes reality, delusion equals clarity.

When fantasy becomes reality, there's no up or down.

No inside and out.

No before and after.

When fantasy becomes reality there's only me and my ego, populating time and space with infantile fixations made real.

My affectations seen as originality.

My defense mechanisms reconstituted as threats coming from outside.

In a self-fulfilling prophecy there's no way to stop.

Welcome to nowhere. Welcome to no time.

Welcome to nobody, ruling the world with an iron fist.

Finding deliverance in obliteration.

Concocting scenarios of triumph, over and over.

Never satisfied, barely conscious.

Of what is this killer vision comprised?

In a false world, everything is false, especially what's seen as true.

And the powers that run this world are false.

And all in it is based on a false premise.

Let's track a crucial element in the vision.

The one which led you to this pass, quaking in your germicidal corner, anxiously misting every available surface with antibacterial spray.

Downing handfuls of pills manufactured from waste products.

Paying through the nose to hasten the time of your demise.

Let's look at a lost chapter in the history of biology.

"If I could live my life over again, I would devote it to proving that germs seek their natural habitat—diseased tissue—rather than being the cause of the diseased tissue; e.g., mosquitoes seek the stagnant water, but do not cause the pool to become stagnant." (Rudolph Virchow)

Pay attention, dear reader, to the correspondences between what follows in the realm of biology and how you and I conceive of threats from the outside world—whether it's blacks or Muslims, AIDS or flu virus, North Koreans or queers.

Whether it's biodiversity or the possibility of a world without betrayal.

Whether it's homeopathy or psychoactive substances.

Please note that, in all cases, someone's fear is being manipulated to someone else's advantage.

Traditional Western medicine teaches and practices the doctrines of Louis Pasteur.

Pasteur's Germ Theory of Disease: fixed species of microbes from an external source invade the body and are the first cause of "infectious" disease.

The concept of unchanging types of bacteria causing specific diseases became officially accepted in late nineteenth-century Europe.

Also called monomorphism, it was adopted by America's medical industry, which took shape at the turn of the last century.

Organized around an American Medical Association formed by drug interests for the purpose of using the legal system—for one example—to destroy the competing homeopathic medical profession.

Controlled by pharmaceutical companies, this industry has become a trillion-dollar-a-year business.

It also includes insurance companies, the FDA, the NIH, the CDC, hospitals, and university research faculties.

(Obviously, many good people work in these organizations, doing many good things, unaware of the nature and degree of manipulation involved in them. But the end result is the same.)

Although those who followed Pasteur drew accurate conclusions from scientific demonstrations, such demonstrations were based on a false premise—

Namely, in order to prove his germ theory, Pasteur used preparations made from diseased tissues of previously sick animals, thus making the injected ones sick.

This gave the appearance that a germ caused the disease, when in fact the preparations themselves were poisonous.

Such a procedure simply demonstrates that you can make people sick by poisoning their blood.

The method of injection by no means duplicating natural "infection."

But Pasteur's ambition wouldn't allow him to see he was confusing a disease with its symptoms.

Now it so happened that another French scientist, Antoine Béchamp, a contemporary of Pasteur's, discovered that infectious symptoms do not arise primarily from external bacterial attacks.

For years, scientists had observed within cells tiny "molecular granulations" whose function was unknown.

Béchamp finally observed that these granules were living fragments.

He renamed them microzymas, "small ferments."

Ferments because they continually change their shape.

These elements exist within all living things and are both the builder and recycler of organisms.

They inhabit cells, blood, and lymph.

Béchamp saw life process as continual cellular breakdown by fermentation, even in a healthy body.

Microzymas are capable of multiplying and reflect either health or disease.

In a state of health they act harmoniously and fermentation occurs beneficially.

In an unbalanced, acidic terrain fermentation is taken over by morbid evolutions including bacteria, yeast, fungus and mold.

They change function, evolving into forms—"germs"—which produce symptoms.

Béchamp developed the concept of pleomorphism, many forms.

He observed granules linking together and "lengthening into bacteria."

Bacteria becomes yeast or fungus, yeast or fungus becomes mold.

Unbalanced terrain.

Disease symptoms.

Putting the two together, we have an explanation of illness completely at odds with Pasteur's germ theory.

Instead of monomorphism, which insists microscopic forms are immutable, Béchamp was seeing constant change.

Once the terrain—which is to say, the blood—becomes overly acidic, these microzymas mutate from small to large, from benign to destructive.

This can be seen under powerful microscopes built by Béchamp's successors, Guenther Enderlein and Gaston Naessens.

But only when live blood is examined.

However, looking at live blood runs counter to the procedure of medical biology, which stains or kills the blood before examining it.

Decades have passed with the evidence of these microscopic transformations readily available.

But most doctors and scientists have refused to look.

(The above material is from *Sick and Tired?* by Robert O. Young.)

And Pasteur—ambitious, politically connected, jealous of Béchamp's genius—mocked and subverted and plagiarized his work.

Until the end of his life, Pasteur denied the validity of pleomorphism, although on his deathbed he was reported to have changed his mind, whispering, "The germ is nothing, the terrain everything."

But by then it was too late.

Too late for what, dear reader?

Too late to view diseases as caused by internal imbalance rather than by invasions from outside.

Too late—but also perfectly understandable, inevitable even.

Because nothing takes place in a vacuum, not even science.

We're talking late nineteenth century, after all.

Hundreds of years into the white man's game of robber baron capitalism and one-dimensional colonialism.

To feed an appetite which knew no bounds and distorted everything.

Within this context, how could life be seen as anything but a ruthless battle between inside and out, between homeland and foreign, between white and colored?

Between rich and poor, civilized and barbaric, free and slave, man and woman?

Between the forces of light and dark, the forces of health and disease?

How could any vision prevail but the fearful, the paranoid, the cruel?

Extirpation the only option.

Multibillion-dollar-per-year defense budgets.

Ceaseless development of technologies destructive beyond imagining.

Beyond all sanity.

Funhouse mirror of us and them.

Horror-movie vision of what comes stalking in the night.

Virus and cancer!

No matter how limitless our pride, our feeling of superiority, deep down we know "they" will outsmart us in the end.

Because they have the unknown on their side.

How to defeat what you can't fully comprehend?

Cancer and virus!

The essence of uncivilized, the embodiment of barbarity—they don't play by the rules.

Cancer multiplies without cease.

A virus is neither living nor dead. It reaches in every direction at once, commandeering one disease after another.

Invasion of the sly, the underhanded.

Lightning quick. Remorseless.

Tricksters without definitive shape or characteristics.

Whereas, in fact, these monsters actually are inversions—negative versions—of the pleomorphic transformations occurring in our own blood.

Betrayal without end!

Microzymas receive chemical signals that the host organism is dead or disorganizing.

Then and only then do they become morbid, their waste products poisoning us from within.

They arise from our being—the humility to accept this, rather than to blame the fictional Other.

(Blame Mother—abandoning me! Switching from the perfect holding environment I trusted as an infant to the threat I sense around me for the rest of my life—betrayal!)

Terrain out of balance.

Morbid forms colonizing the body reflect—and are reflected by, which came first?—the predatory agendas of transnational corporations, today's colonial powers.

Acid colors of high fashion wash into the gutters of sullen cityscapes.

While above such unseemly chaos, the victors ride in armored helicopters, treating themselves to the last of the world's beluga.

Turning to one another with burning glances, relishing their roles in the drama.

Luxuriousness and high-tech attention to detail reinforcing their sense of security.

Reinforcing the illusion that they're in charge.

The class system itself a terrain out of balance.

Distortion of master and slave, of nobility and commoner, of CEO and employee.

"Power" always meaning power over something concrete, over someone specific.

Always biographical, never abstract.

Always to be seen in terms of who, what, where.
Whose life empowered, whose prospects stifled?
Whose desires quenched, whose heart deadened?
And to be seen in the vision of a life lived for myself only.
When I'm sick I turn to antibiotics, further compromising my terrain.
Antibiotics which don't really kill bacteria, they simply force them into nastier stages of their life cycle.
Eventually resulting in more serious symptoms.
Untreatable strains of bacteria, super-resistant "germs."
The Germ Theory—what a way to spend one's life!
Is the trade-off worth it?
The trade-off between greed and sharing?
Between deviousness and directness?
Between rational and intuitive?
Between the chosen people and cultural cornucopia?
Between dead food and live, between acid and alkaline?
Between clutching and letting go?
Between rock-solid ego and wide-open space?

"When you look at your mind, you see that its essential nature is emptiness. But this does not make your mind nonexistent, or make your body a corpse. Because while the nature of your mind is emptiness, it also has a natural characteristic of cognitive lucidity, and this cognitive lucidity is inseparable from the emptiness which is its fundamental nature. Although the mind is empty in the sense of being devoid of any kind of substantial existence, it nevertheless is the ground for all of the qualities of buddhahood and for all of the confusion of samsara."

("Pointing Out the Dharmakaya," Thrangu Rinpoche in *Shenpen Ösel*)

Visions of emptiness taken for real:
Lowly English plantain envisioned as a weed, remorselessly erad-

WORLD<small>ON</small>FIRE

icated with herbicides which foul my drinking water.

Deer in the meadow my mortal enemy, slain to keep him from my flower beds.

Laughing child my corporation's de facto employee, chained to a filthy machine halfway around the world for pennies a day.

Pregnant mother beaten and beheaded, her corpse raped by soldiers trained by my country's military.

The disconnect immense, proliferating everywhere—

Hydroelectric dams flooding canyons and mountains, drowning out villages, forcing farmers into the slums of megacities.

The morbid energies of "advanced" nations, competing with one another to sell killer technologies to the highest bidder.

American teenagers, glassy-eyed and taciturn, inheritors of the greatest civilization on Earth.

Watch them as they cruise through strip-mall wastelands, drowning in a sea of junk food and sugar, their bodies sludge-filled before the age of twenty.

Their spirits precancerous, their minds lost in trance.

Mighty rivers turned to sewer water for buckets of gold, for barrels of gasoline nobody knows they don't even need.

Ancient forests demolished in a matter of weeks for chopsticks.

But I've told you the story of the chopsticks already, haven't I?

Perhaps I'm starting to bore you?

No doubt you have a clever way to make everything come right again.

I'll leave you to your own devices, you sad-faced amnesiac.

Why am I trying to be such a good bodhisattva?

Maybe I have better things to do with my time.

So fuck you.

And the terrible horse you rode in on.

(Gosh, such hostility toward the reader! What's that all about? Maybe I'm conflating him/her with someone I've known in the past, someone toward whom I have hateful feelings. An old girlfriend, perhaps? Co-workers or bosses, political figures, storied villains?

Or how about Dad?

Ouch . . . The colonial impulse in a family setting, far from the prying eyes of the rest of humanity.

How about when the front door closes and the porch light goes out? The candles gutter in their antique brass sticks. The pets hide under the sofa. There's a sound of strangled weeping that leaks from the kitchen like a plague—secret folk song of Mom dutifully preparing dinner. There's a pale watercolor of Sister sitting alone at the edge of the bed in her room, silently staring into space, seeing nothing. There's a thin white column of smoke, perfectly straight, which hits the ceiling in my room and breaks apart. Smoke of my spirit with nowhere to go. There's Dad, a tumbler of scotch in his hand, pacing back and forth after a hard day's work, unconscious of the rage which spirals up inside him like a snake. Too easy to call him a caged animal. Would that he were! Would that we all—no matter how confined—at least had memories of unboundedness. Of totality.)

Wrinkled snapshot from the late forties, how difficult it is for me to look at you.

Where's the vanished life you instantly recall?

My father on a hillside in Pennsylvania, smiling and black-haired, virile in a tight-fitting T-shirt as he holds me in his arms.

And sitting on his chest, my little hands around his neck, I'm smiling too.

At that moment the whole world is smiling, completed, sure of itself, at ease.

Now I see who my father really was.

The brilliant spark of his preciousness.

I remember his integrity.

I remember him providing for us, giving us shelter and security, tomorrow the same as today, today the same as yesterday.

How I respected him then, how I looked forward to his presence.

What went wrong?

Young man buried inside the hectoring bully he later became.

Young man misplacing the thread of his being, turning into the fallen angel, suspicious and vengeful, scheming to control a world full of dark challenges.

A world mirroring his lack of belief in his own essence.

Life's adventure become mere drudgery.

Trapped inside a marriage he no longer wanted.

Making my mother suffer.

Neither of them tasting the joy they once knew.

And what about me?

I have to separate the good father from my physical father.

No longer internalizing him, no longer rejecting him, no longer projecting him onto other people.

I have to allow his essential qualities to reveal themselves in me.

Powerful and delicate all at once.

Intelligent and capable and free.

Able to deal with the world.

5.

I'm alone again.

Just like on the morning you up and left me.

You slammed shut the cabin door and marched off toward a lime-green and magenta sky, balancing a burger in one hand and a cell phone in the other.

Determined to have your fun, come what may.

Suddenly hating me because I had opened your eyes.

Telling you about the year 2012 and the Mayan prophecy of a paradigm shift bringing an end to these Dark Ages.

In fact, already upon us, my darling.

But you had no clue.

How dare I break apart your dream?

How dare I point out to you the wells, fresh out of oil, pumping genetically altered human blood into the sky?

How dare I show you the endless vista of rusted automobiles, the melted highways, the crumbling skyscrapers?

This was nothing but a flood of hateful revenge!

I must have had such a twisted childhood, you said, to distort everything, to take out my resentment on the innocent world around me.

Look, you insisted, your voice rising with emotion.

Can't you see the cars speeding along the freeways as always?

Can't you see the lights twinkling in cities without end?

Can't you see the caravans of trucks, rumbling back and forth on their mission of full and empty, always on schedule, never missing a beat?

And the people, you said.

Try to look at them with unbiased eyes.

See how happy they are, not just here in the good old U.S.A., but change the channel, peer into Bucharest or Mombasa or São Paulo.

What about Scotland or Cambodia or Mozambique?

Everyone's doing what they've always done, fooling around and falling in love, having babies and raising kids, going to work and coming home, eating dinner, playing in the yard, singing in the rain.

Listen to them, you asshole.

Listen to their timeless human melody, rich and clear, always the same.

How dare you even think that it's coming to an end?

"You perverse bastard," you hissed.

Then all your attention was taken up by chewing on your burger, by chattering into your cell phone.

Stubborn hallucination, wondrous in its staying power.

But I knew you well.

I could sense as you walked away that you were wavering in your allegiance to this rotting dream.

If only you'd steer clear of the trance for a second longer, maybe you'd have a change of heart.

So I followed you further into the wilderness.

But then a man appeared on the desert floor a few yards away from you.

His hand cradled a cell phone.

His jaws worked furiously on indigestible rubber.

The moment you saw him you smiled.

And right before my eyes the two of you turned into four, the four into sixteen, the sixteen into 156, the 156 into 24,366, the 24,366 into 59,370,195.

And that's how I lost track of you, my darling.

Now I can't even remember your name.

But anyway, what's in a name?

Something Mom and Dad chuckle over, high on crack cocaine,

determined to put their bad habits behind them now that they have someone else to live for.

This beautiful baby they call their very own.

What more can we do but shrug our shoulders and wish them luck?

Because no matter how steep the odds, at least she still has a name and not a number.

At least she's born from human flesh and not from a petri dish.

Is she the last in the series?

Because if there was a first there must be a last.

Nothing goes on forever, not even "forever."

The sky's a dancing inverted lentil of space.

A transparent petri dish.

Outside it is the unknown, and the unknown doesn't have a name.

Or would you rather be voice-activated, your memories worn in a bar code on your sleeve?

Suffice only a new bar code for a sparkling fresh set of memories.

Ah, the malleability of memory!

In a culture of avoidance, what better way to triumph over childhood traumas than to erase them?

A protein fix to obliterate bad memories.

But the scientists working long nights in their sterilized chambers have forgotten something.

Trauma leads to negative appraisals of self and world, and these appraisals then exist independent of the memories which helped form them.

Negative appraisals of self and world—doesn't that describe the very realm we've created, the realm in which we're enfolded?

The way a sound is enfolded in light years of silence.

Or a shadow briefly crosses a mirror deep inside a dream.

That shadow has a name.

A mother and father.

A childhood somewhere which—without warning—opens up one day beneath the shadow's feet.

An abyss through which the shadow falls endlessly.

And no amount of supplication, argument, fear, rage, despair, drugs, sex, alcohol, violence, can set the shadow on solid ground again.

Solid ground . . .

The Earth, treated with such disdain by warped brain power, takes her revenge in the only way possible.

Deliverance into a realm without support, without weight, without touch.

Without smell or taste.

A realm dubbed "virtual."

A realm seemingly new but actually primal.

Because being lost never changes.

Lost in space the mind sees itself reflected in the sky.

A transparent, inverted petri dish.

Directionless. Atemporal. Disconnected.

Which is the mind and which is the sky?

And no matter how loud the scream, nothing is heard.

No matter how intense the longing, nothing is felt.

No matter how deep the conviction, nothing is conveyed.

Nothing except the ability to change memories, shapes, identities, with the speed of light.

"Contrary to everything that seems obvious and 'natural,' nature's first creatures were immortal. It was only by obtaining the power to die, by dint of constant struggle, that we became the living beings we are today. Blindly we dream of overcoming death through immortality, when all the time immortality is the most horrific of possible fates. Encoded in the earliest of our cells, this fate is now reappearing on our horizons, so to speak, with the advent of cloning.

"The evolution of the biosphere is what drives immortal beings to become mortal ones. They move, little by little, from the absolute continuity found in the subdivision of the same—in bacteria— toward the possibility of birth and death. Next, the egg becomes fertilized by a sperm and specialized sex cells make their appearance. The resulting entity is no longer a copy of either one of the pair that engendered it: rather, it is a new and singular combination.

"But the game isn't over yet, and reversion is always possible. It can be found . . . in the enormous enterprise we living beings ourselves undertake today: a project to reconstruct a homogeneous and uniformly consistent universe—an artificial continuum this time— that unfolds within a technological and mechanical medium, extending over our vast information network, where we are in the process of building a perfect clone, an identical copy of our world, a virtual artifact that opens up the prospect of endless reproduction.

"It is argued that there is nothing to fear from bio-genetically engineered cloning, because whatever happens, culture will continue to differentiate us. Salvation lies in our acquirements: culture alone will preserve us from the hell of the Same.

"In fact, exactly the reverse is true. It is culture that clones us, and mental cloning anticipates any biological cloning. It is the matrix of acquired traits that, today, clones us culturally under the sign of monothought."

(*The Vital Illusion*, Jean Baudrillard)

Wow, how spooked-out can you get?

Hail our techno-eugenic future!

Wearing his new designer genes, bionic man leads the way.

Reinventing life at the genetic level so it fits the techno-system.

The goal, to create a severed humanity.

Two classes—the genetically rich and their underclass service providers.

But wait a second—the threat of human genetic engineering may be nothing more than a red herring (the original GMO?).

Because isn't an underclass pretty much already in place?

Isn't the citizen adapted to work in corporations—intelligent, time-serving, conformist—on the job today?

Clone as metaphor, as conceptual prop for what's here.

In every society, cosmologies serve a rationalizing function.

How is our cosmology, "The Information Age," serving us?

"With living organisms, as with computers, information capacity and time constraints become primary considerations.

"Much of the new thinking about evolution parallels the new way commerce is being organized in the network-based global economy.

"Living beings are no longer perceived as birds and bees, foxes and hens, but as bundles of genetic information. Life becomes a code to be deciphered."

(*The Biotech Century*, Jeremy Rifkin)

Fortunately, however, nature's secrets are stubbornly elusive.

The Human Genome Project may prove to be an expensive washout.

Contradictions and limitations abound.

Because gene tests are unreliable in predicting what will happen to an actual person.

"As has been pointed out by many scientists, most diseases are complex, and correlations between genes and diseases are therefore weak. Associations between a disease and a 'genetic marker' (of unknown function) can occur by chance and some have proved to be spurious. Searches for susceptibility genes have been more successful, but these account for less than three percent of all cases.

"The growth in 'bioinformatics' is an admission of the vast realms of ignorance that separate the 100,000 genes in the human genome from the living human being. There is no simple linear causal chain connecting a gene to a trait, good or bad. Behind the hype is a desperate attempt to turn the exponentially increasing amount of information into knowledge that can pay off the heavy investments already sunk into the project.

"The overwhelming causes of ill-health are environmental and social. That is the conclusion of a growing body of research. The genetic deterministic approach is pernicious because it diverts attention and resources away from addressing the real causes of ill-health, while at the same time stigmatizing the victims and fueling eugenic tendencies in society."

("The Human Genome Sellout," Mae-Wan Ho, in *Third World Resurgence*)

But the Human Genome Project's success isn't necessary for shotgun procedures to continue.

Like xenotransplantation—crossing the human/animal barrier with viruses.

Genetic diversity suddenly the highest priority.

Indigenous people the prime target, their genes the most precious because of their uniqueness.

Terra nullis—colonization's doctrine that the land is empty, underutilized by the savages who inhabit it.

Giving us the excuse to move in and take over.

As now we're taking over bodies, cells, genes.

Bio-colonialism without accountability or liability.

Biological samples collected and stored in gene banks without consent.

By 1999, the three leading human genomics corporations had filed in excess of three million EST (expressed sequence tag) patent claims.

The public at large mystified and silent.

But the subjects aren't all taking it lying down.

"We'll meet them with our spears and arrows." (Tribe in the Philippines)

"Everything about me biologically is connected to place." (Paiute Indian)

So the smart money's backing away from the Human Genome Project.

Only to resurface in nanotechnology and in satellites and sensors.

A critical mass of investment capital.

Major patent holders—the U.S. Navy, the U.S. Army, Exxon, Boeing, 3M, BASF, Bayer, IBM.

And what is nanotechnology?

Pay attention, dear reader.

That hummingbird outside your bedroom window.

Those houseflies interrupting your closed-door meeting on the forty-third floor.

Where did they come from?

What are they doing?

"Nanotechnology is to inanimate matter what biotech is to animate matter.

"Simply put, a nano is one-billionth of a meter, an atom-sized bit of flotsam that can snuggle inside almost anything. In commercial terms, nanotech is the manufacture and (most important and difficult) the *replication* of machinery and end products that have been constructed from the atom up."

("The ETC Century," Pat Roy Mooney, in *Development Dialogue*)

What might nanotech do?

That is, what are its developers aiming at?

"There is virtually no area of social activity or economic production that will not be affected by nanotechnology. In a bionic world where nanotech and biotech merge, we will see nano-scale biocomputers and biosensors able to monitor everything from plant regulators to political rallies."

According to its proponents, nanotech offers an end to disease as we know it, the elimination of the aging process, the eradication of air and water pollution, the end of hunger, the cessation of reliance on fossil fuels, the creation of heretofore unknown wealth.

"All this sounds like the early days and dreams of nuclear energy, when those advocating the 'peaceful use of the atom' predicted a limitless source of clean energy that would transform the world. Nanotechnology also proposes the peaceful use of the atom as the building block for construction. Some analysts are projecting somewhat similar negative complications.

"Self-replicating nanobots capable of geometrically accelerating production of incredibly durable (and invisible) machinery could cause immense damage. What if the nanobots cannot be stopped? What of the implications for military purposes and terrorism—especially state terrorism? The same nano-medicine that can fight a virus can also become a virus. Indeed, the very power of nanotechnology to accomplish all things physical inexpensively and inexhaustibly, is also its threat. Nanotech may lend credence to the claim of governments that they must control society in order to safeguard the application of the technology.

"At the beginning of 1999, *The Economist* magazine reported on the work of three nanotech-style research institutes to develop micro air vehicles as attack and/or surveillance aircraft. One prototype known as the Black Widow, under development at Aeroenvironment, a U.S. company, has actually managed to get airborne. It is fifteen centimeters (six inches) in diameter, can fly through apartment windows at about forty-five km/h, stay aloft for sixteen minutes, and carry back recorded images. In Mainz, Germany, the Institute for Microtech has developed a micro-helicopter only one inch long and weighing less than one hundredth of an ounce." (Pat Roy Mooney)

Self-replicating nanobots . . .

Thank you and have a great day.

But there's more on the stove, dear reader.

Research in neurosciences bridging biology and informatics.

Focus on the nervous system at the molecular and cellular level.

"Commercial and military enthusiasm is highest for 'pattern recognition' in the development of neural networks. Neural networks could marshal New York's traffic system, or eavesdrop on (and understand) all the telephone conversations of an entire country. Canada, together with the U.K., U.S.A., New Zealand, and Australia, has established the Echelon satellite communications monitoring system that already allows their intelligence agencies to simultaneously monitor hundreds of thousands of international phone conversations and select out those using specific words and phrases."

Your call is important to us . . .

"Although Human Performance Enhancement is properly a subset of neurosciences, this field comes with a unique moral burden including slavery and eugenics. Two breakthroughs in brain imaging . . . make it possible to determine what part of the brain does what.

"In short, neuroscientists are developing strategies that could manipulate the interests and skills of workers (including soldiers) and that could also reduce the need for workers, if the so-called 'man/machine' interface with cognitive neural networks makes management of complex industrial and agricultural systems realistic.

"If you can do this, you can also win elections—or do away with 'democracy' altogether." (Pat Roy Mooney)

Astounding, the lengths to which tranced-out self-starters will go to exercise control.

But they forget one thing—their technology can attach itself only to those who buy into it.

Only to those of like mind.

Because what doesn't kill me makes me stronger.

Locales always have outlasted empires.

"Without legitimacy, power structures crumble." (A. Gramsci)

And this bastard structure's days are numbered.

This age of manufactured mind.

This push to transform life into products.

This culture drowning the present in the name of the future.

This heart of darkness beating its fluid into every cell.

Flooding everything but the "American business" version of the bottom line.

Throw someone in jail for breaking a McDonald's window, but not whoever's responsible for the wage the person is paid to work there.

Throw the landless in jail for squatting on a patch of weeds, but not whoever's responsible for the forests cut down around them.

Give an Earth Liberation Front activist twenty-two years in prison for torching three SUVs, but ignore the "property rights" of all other life-forms.

Market prices the sole arbiter of value.

Every choice made on the basis of economic return.

Human life calculated as earning potential.

Tank cars full of privatized water and not a drop to drink.

Diabolique

Speaking of the Devil, who is he anyway?

Present-tense question, because eighty percent of Americans believe in his existence.

Eighty percent pray to God to protect them from the Devil's predations.

Eighty percent ask God to show them the way to right conduct.

Far be it from me to pull rank on these good people.

After all, they're the ones who make up consensus reality's actual flesh-and-blood majority.

Not some spin doctor in his computer tower.

Not some covey of time-card academics deciding for us what we think.

No, I'll lay my money on the intuition of the four out of five.

They're quite clear about the Devil.

The Prince of Darkness, incarnation of evil, is fully active right now.

He's available anytime of the day or night for Faustian bargains to be struck.

Your land in exchange for the oil underneath it, your crops for sterile seeds which mortgage away your future, your health for a sack of deathcamp glueburgers.

Your job, family security, and sense of self-worth exchanged for an abstract game of currency trading.

Sounds like the Devil's work, doesn't it?

But who is he, really?

He came to this land on the Mayflower, we know that much.

There was no Devil before the Puritans arrived.

Trickster spirits, yes, dark energies which needed to be placated, ancestor presences causing all sorts of havoc if not respected. But the Devil? No.

Irony worthy of the Evil One himself, to ascribe his own ways to the very people who were living here before repressed palefaces took over the landscape.

The spiritual practices of the Indians, their sexual mores, their communal existence—how clever to call all this the work of the Devil!

Ask the Hopi if there was Original Sin.

Ask the Chippewa if God threw us out of Paradise because we listened to a snake with a bad-news gleam in his eye.

Ask the Maya if a serpent seduced their first woman, tempting her with knowledge of the Tree of Good and Evil.

And that she corrupted the first man with her feminine wiles, bringing disaster on the heads of their progeny forevermore.

But it's certain that the Devil piloted slave ships which landed on the shores of Caribbean sugar plantations.

He slaughtered Plains Indians by the tens of thousands to make this land safe for the Iron Horse.

He invented biological warfare on these shores.

When the smallpox vaccine was developed, the U.S. Army inoculated soldiers and then traded smallpox-infected blankets with the Indians.

He brought mosquitoes and rats and alcohol and tuberculosis to the jungle islands of the Pacific and then carpeted them with golf courses.

He sneaked into American universities with the aid of the CIA, disguised as German nuclear scientists on the run from a collapsing Nazi regime.

He fed LSD to unsuspecting prisoners as part of research programs to melt down enemy minds.

He universalized the very concept of the enemy, expanding it to include everyone and everything.

He made war on Iraq in order to further American oil interests, declining to liberate that country from its own Beelzebub after he had bombed its children into dust.

He suckered researchers into believing that all technological advance is morally neutral.

He stole your time, giving you dollar bills in return.

His finger in every pie, his hand on every ass, his word in every glib rationalization, his glance lighting up every madhouse window.

But the moment you look for him he's not there.

If you ask him to stand and face you he's gone.

What Devil?

How crude, how déclassé to even mention such a personage.

Of course you're speaking metaphorically, my dear.

Who would take you seriously otherwise?

But I've seen the Devil in action, I know he exists.

I've smelled his presence, unlike any other—choking fumes in the middle of Paradise.

I've heard the sound of his triumph—the machinery deafening and unrelenting, never pausing, never resting, twenty-four hours a day, seven days a week.

In October, 2000, I traveled to the jungles of Ecuador.

I met Huaorani men, from a tribe of no more than a couple hundred souls.

They were seduced and browbeaten into working for the oil companies which are everywhere down there these days.

Indoctrinated into a money economy for which they previously had no use, the men abandon their wives and children for the cheap thrills of liquor and venereal disease.

The Evil One snaps his fingers—men are transformed from proud inhabitants of the forest into ghostly versions of themselves.

The Evil One has them sign legal documents—the rights to their land are snatched away.

He creates a vacuum within which the women step, magically transformed from self-sufficient cultivators of manioc and papaya into prostitutes for the oil camps.

And not only the Huaorani.

The Shuar, the Secoya, the Quichua—all are rapidly being pushed into lives of degradation, their villages no more than stage sets for ecotourists whose dollars go mostly to preening macho guides from the towns.

Throughout the jungles of the Oriente roads have been laid in every direction.

Running beside them are black steel pipes full of blood.

The Vampire sucks this blood from beneath the forest floor while his compatriots clear-cut the trees above, shipping tropical hardwood to Europe, the United States, and Japan.

Oil and timber and gold.

Syphilis and alcoholism and AIDS.

Trinkets and batteries and cigarettes.

For centuries now, fortunes deposited in distant cities of the world.

And in exchange, torture and starvation.

Not to mention the mirage of consumer addiction, the friendly fascism of television.

So don't tell me that the Devil's just a metaphor.

Don't pretend that such an elusive yet all-powerful force is imaginary, a product of superstition.

Because the joke's on you, dear reader.

Very soon—tomorrow—today—you too will wake up with a tube in your neck, your life force sucked out into the void for someone else's profit.

What delusion, to persist in thinking that "no one" is doing this to you.

Rage—how can I control it?

What good does it do me?

My chest constricted, my heart heavy, I returned from Ecuador and wandered the streets of the world capital, unable to relax, unable to savor the finest wines, unable to eat elaborate meals prepared by temperamental geniuses of the jaded palate.

My friends insisted I dine with them—"You can't imagine what you're missing!" they whispered, afraid others were going to steal our table from under our noses—and I forced some famous seafood sausage down my throat.

Ten minutes later I was puking in an elegant restaurant bathroom, my stomach convulsing, hydrochloric acid searing my lips.

But my friends barely noticed my absence.

They were scheming among themselves to raise the four hundred dollars more it would take to taste that bottle of Special Reserve they'd had their eye on for months.

"This night of all nights!" they shouted, frustrated in spite of gullets already stuffed with delicacies beyond description.

I stumbled outside, leaving them to their exquisite addiction.

Walking slowly, with measured steps, I disassociated.

Traffic sounds, people passing on the sidewalk, the weather, the buildings—all of it meant nothing to me.

The only thing that mattered, the only thing I saw, was my treasured mental picture of Pego, the seventy-five-year-old Huaorani warrior I'd met in Ecuador.

Not more than five feet tall with jet black hair, his blowgun balanced on his shoulder, he came alive when we ventured into the forest.

He paused before one plant after another, clucking to himself like a bird as he described its uses.

This one for snakebite, that one for menstrual problems, another for intestinal pain.

As we penetrated the layers of green, a profusion of butterflies and other insects buzzed and floated around our heads.

Lattices of birdsong filled the air.

Pego often paused, smiling joyfully as he tilted his head into the canopy above.

He uttered some word in Huaorani and our guide would translate ("X bird, Y tree") but it was obvious that the name of what he saw was only the beginning of his engagement with it.

No matter what we jotted in our notebooks, we could not follow him into that engagement.

His radiant smile, his gentle satisfaction.

Soon I put away my notebook and just watched him.

The only time his smile vanished was when someone among our little group took out a camera and pointed it in his direction.

Then our guide told us, "Pego was a feared warrior in his youth. He killed many people. In fact, as recently as four years ago he was still leading raiding parties on neighboring Huaorani villages. It was their practice to kill the women, even though there are less than five hundred Huaorani left. It meant nothing to Pego when I explained how they were sabotaging their own future by murdering potential mothers. He said that this was the custom of their people. This was the way it always had been."

And the custom of our people?

Is it equally harebrained, equally self-destructive in spite of how right it feels?

(How right it must have felt to Pego, esteemed by his brothers for his prowess with the blowgun. Alive with anticipation as he threaded his way through the forest night toward unsuspecting victims.)

Is it the custom of our people to burn holes in the ozone which protects us from harmful radiation?

Is it the custom of our people to pollute the aquifers on which we depend for drinking water?

Is it the custom of our people to treat the diversity of forests as nothing more than potential board feet?

To look at the broad Earth as potential strip mines?

We have no choice, we say.

"I'm doing this to put bread on the table. I'm doing this for my career, for my survival."

How can it be, our time on this planet passed in brittle, envious competition?

How is it possible that our hunger for survival has become the principal agent of our destruction?

"Destruction?" you echo, sarcastic and uncomprehending.

"What destruction? Look at the lives we Americans lead! Look at the breathtaking medical advances of the past century. Look at our safe drinking water, our fabulous gleaming kitchens. Look at our big fat automobiles. Look at the sweet vacations we can take—to Aruba, Curaçao, Martinique. The beaches are just what the doctor ordered. We return to civilization refreshed, energized, ready to tackle the business of the day with gusto. Ready to move mountains of money around with lightning speed. Ready to scheme our way to the top of our respective institutions. Ready to bring our transnational tabula rasa into every last village on the globe. After all, this is our custom. It's the way we've always lived, only more high-powered than before. Can you imagine the thrill we get, admired by our team as we score one point after another? If all of this could be explained to him, of course Pego would be proud of us. Of course he would understand. It's only you who's out of step. Only you who are some sort of stick-in-the-mud subverter . . ."

Call me names if you like, but the facts remain—your Dad dying of cancer at sixty-five, your wife lopsided on Prozac, your kids petulant balloons, vitriolic yet helpless.

Your life's fish tank a Möbius-strip vista of degraded landscapes projected on ever-larger TV screens.

With ever-greater visual definition.

With more and more realistic sound.

So realistic you can't tell anymore when the TV's on and when the TV's off.

Are you really taken in by the following?

"NEW IBM ThinkPad Notebooks," the ad in your local newspaper announces.

"IT'S LIKE LIFE WITHOUT RESTRICTIONS. Work when you want—where you want. And don't forget to play."

And what's the fine print say?

"Tired of playing by the rules? Don't do this and you can't do that. IBM ThinkPad notebooks let you bend some of the rules, and still get the work done right. Work from the hammock at midnight, with the help of your ThinkLight keyboard light. Or pull out your optional . . . Surprise your boss with . . . Or pop out your second hard drive and . . . Choose to do it all running as fast as you need."

And how fast is that?

You're pretty sharp—don't you see how this ad manipulates and insults you?

How it's one cog in a slick machine constructed to lead you around by the nose?

How it mocks everything your spirit holds dear?

Life without restrictions . . .

Don't forget to play . . .

Tired of playing by the rules . . .

Yes, you're a rebel all right—late at night in your dreams.

But the amazing thing is, you're actually well aware of how advertisements work.

You *do* understand.

Empire's most staggering achievement is to make you feel savvy while continuing to milk you.

It values above all that knowing smile you have when you look in the mirror.

Nobody can pull the wool over your eyes, right?

What about trading in your SUV for a newer, higher-riding one? Won't that be cool?

What about coming after me with a tire iron?

Here's that bearer of bad news again—bash his teeth in, string him up.

That'll solve the problem.

Or maybe you still think there is no problem?

As long as the ball scores keep rolling in, as long as some unlooked-for dalliance presents itself to your little ego dickie now and then. As long as the gasoline keeps pouring in.

But that's been explained already—you're living an airtight collective hallucination.

There is no gasoline.

It stopped flowing this morning, remember?

Why do I have to keep reminding you?

It's gone—along with your job, your family, your "way of life."

In reality you're not riding around bored and queasy and querulous—you're cowering stark naked in a filthy shack in the middle of nowhere.

Nobody told you it would end like this, did they?

They promised you the world while ripping you off from day one.

Now you know. Only now it's one day too late.

All you have left is your breath.

You'd better follow that.

Breathe slowly.

In and out. In and out.

That's it.

6.

Until unlabored breathing eventually brings an effortless existence.
Naturally occurring timeless awareness.
Buddha nature.
A Golden Age!
It's as old as the hills and as close as the space around us.
A time out of mind with no separation anxiety, no Oedipus complex.
No leaky gut syndrome, no heart disease.
No drug addiction, no self-hatred.
No autistic hall of mirrors, no serial killers.
No rampaging ego, no banks filled with filthy lucre, no soldiers to defend them.
No highways covered with racing automatons, no dioxin saturating the food chain.
No assembly-line slaughterhouses, stretching as far as the heart can see.
No genetic phantoms crowding out the flower of nature's intelligence.
No media mirages unthinking multitudes take for real.
No interactive infomercials concocted by ravenous corporations—the new Jealous Gods.
No speeding faster and faster to a death all alone and terrified.

Speed, rocket fuel of my youth.
Once upon a time I worshipped you, little pink and yellow pills, dysoxin and all the rest whose names I forget—fallout of the sixties indeed, brain cells vaporized into thin air.

The victims, the waste—tell me about that tomorrow.

Fly now, pay later.

And crystal methedrine, which left all other chemicals in the dust.

I remember licking at your bitter powder then staying up for days, wired beyond compare, gabbing and scribbling nonstop, fused to the energy of the sun.

Crystal methedrine I pounded the pavements of San Francisco for you, 1967, heart booming, brain on fire.

Unable to stop walking for miles, for hours, my jaw clenching uncontrollably.

And for what?

Fly now, pay later.

The needle . . . I shot up only once, with the aforementioned charismatic poet, in the winter of 1972. (Putative source of my hep C?)

And stayed up all night furiously writing a new poem.

A poem which dismayed my friends because it had none of the carefree invention of my work until then.

None of the subtlety, none of the grace.

That poem—self-involved, simplistic—I couldn't see for what it was.

Speed made me sloppy, made me cocky.

My velocity had altered, and with it my perception.

Perception meaning perception of the universe.

Speed, dear reader, and cocaine and computers and the cell phone—you still think they're unrelated?

You believe they came out of nowhere?

And modafinil, the newest wonder drug, sustaining poised and productive alertness for days on end with no detectable side effects.

To whose benefit?

Ah, you say, I'm making too big a jump.

From "speed kills" to the glories of online banking—it's too extreme.

What are my sources, where are my footnotes?

But all you have to do is reflect—what was life like in times past?

At what pace did it move?

How did the space between people resonate?

How often and for how long were laborers expected to "show up" on the job?

The concept of work itself—in what ways is it different now?

The ailments which people suffer from then and now, how do they vary?

How to explain our current obsession with illness?

Our unending payout for medical insurance?

Our fear of skyrocketing disease rates?

The quality of life, has that altered for better or worse?

Ascertain for me, dear reader, the amount of psychic free space available to people today.

Show me someone who's not trapped inside schedules, who's not always looking at his/her watch, and I'll show you an antiquated personality ill-adapted to present-day life.

A misfit.

A freak.

Meanwhile, children morph into teens bent over violent video games, supersonic hyperactivity bred in the service of abstract slaughter.

And adolescents, after a suitable period sowing wild oats, are poured into the mold of the rest of their lives.

Many find themselves without job security, while the fortunate work for the big corporations.

Riding back and forth on traffic-choked "freeways."

"It gets worse every year," we say with a heroic grimace.

Back and forth from point A to point B, our mental space cluttered with more tasks each year, the interval at which we're expected to complete them decreasing, the downtime more and more elusive.

Speed kills indeed.

Compression packing our options into smaller and smaller units, into tighter and tighter corners.

Harry Houdini, a taste of things to come for everyone.

Remember the great magician, tied up in steel cables and tossed into the sea? Handcuffed and sealed inside an airtight container? Buried alive?

Remember the fascination with his exploits?

How did he escape? Why didn't he suffocate and die? How did he do it?

How indeed?

And how will we do it?

Only we're not onstage and nobody's watching us.

Although not so long ago, for a few precious years, some thought they'd slipped out of their manacles.

Ah, the sixties—don't start me talkin', I'll tell everything I know.

I'll show you promise evaporate like morning dew.

The sixties—what happened?

From the Diggers distributing free food on San Francisco streets to Keith Richards dressed in a Gestapo uniform, thumbing his nose at a full-length mirror in dead of night.

From intentional communities springing up around the country to Richard Nixon's secret glee at a generation stoned to the gills, unable to act.

(Listening to the real White House tapes, we hear his inimitable voice: "Well, the hippies are finished. That was easy. Now how about blindsiding the niggers with all that Asian heroin the Company has stashed away? And we'll throw more television at everybody else.")

Don't start me talkin'.

May 1968 in Paris—I was there.

Flashbacks from the final European revolution.

Chased by riot police up corkscrew apartment-house stairways.

Tearing cobblestones from underfoot to build tear-gas soaked barricades.

Wandering the halls of the Sorbonne at all hours of the day and night, surrounded by crowds of wide-eyed students, workers, bourgeoisie—everybody preternaturally awake, laughing and embracing, their separation cast aside—for how long?

And crammed into a red velvet box at the liberated Théâtre Odéon, I looked down at the stage where an open mike was offered to whoever wanted to speak.

No matter that the rhetoric droning from below was by turns

moving and fatuous—all of us in that little plush box had tears in our eyes.

I turned to the old couple beside me.

In a trembling voice the woman said, "This makes me so proud. Being here tonight connects me to 1870. To 1848. To 1789."

And a hundred thousand workers marching noisily along the boulevards.

The police powerless to intervene.

Unable to take back control of the Sorbonne.

Unable to stop masses of people from assembling.

Until an afternoon came when it really seemed as if the structure would collapse.

As if, at any moment, all the strands of resistance would come together and—

But then something utterly eerie took place.

I entered the courtyard of the Sorbonne and almost no one was there. Graffiti-covered statues and walls looked back at me in silence.

The trash-strewn streets were empty.

Then one by one, vans filled with troops appeared, deploying in every direction, taking over.

Because weeks before, when the State bowed to a greater force and withdrew, a vacuum had been created.

A vacuum without a coherent vision which could fill it.

So that after the rage for freedom had spent itself, the State reasserted its authority.

And its structure once more securely locked in place.

(After that, for the first time, I saw video cameras affixed to lampposts along the major thoroughfares.)

Somewhere sometime this whole mirage first solidified.

Somewhere sometime it rose out of the desert, shuddering into focus, drawing a line in the sand.

Leaving a shadow where before there had been only bright open space.

But we don't like hearing that with private property came separation, even though what could be more obvious?

We don't like hearing that before agriculture and domestic animals—before herds and storehouses—there was no wealth to defend.

As simple as that.

Because without wealth to defend, we're brothers and sisters—no more, no less.

Without wealth to defend, without boundary lines, without hierarchy and caste and enforced mediation, we're connected to creation.

After all these centuries, in one moment we re-enter the Golden Age.

We wake up to our own divine essence.

We recapture the Garden and toss out the Jealous God who presumes to dictate the terms of our existence.

Finally tasting time again as an ally, we resume wandering.

And immediately our egos soften.

And the monsters on which they feed disappear.

Ah, but I see your doubtful smile, dear reader.

I'm jumping the gun, aren't I?

Clock time still holds us in thrall.

(So near and yet so far.)

But for sure we can return to the source of the problem.

This conversion of life's myriad richness into one thing and one thing only—the bottom line.

From *Archeology of Violence* by the great political anthropologist Pierre Clastres—

"How can it be that the majority obeys a single person, not only obeys him but serves him, not only serves him but wants to serve him?"

(For a contemporary feel, substitute "corporation" for "single person.")

This is Étienne de la Boétie's question from the sixteenth century, asked when he was only eighteen years old, which Clastres uses as a jumping-off point to examine the birth of political power and the State.

The birth of caste, of law, of coercion.

Ah, yes—how can it be?

How is it that we moderns reject Western religion, yet cling to Judeo-Christianity's biggest myth?

The myth that life must be suffering.

That slavish work is preordained, inescapable.

In fact, we're more bamboozled than the faithful, who at least have an explanation for their plight.

What explanation do we have?

"That's life . . . The way things are . . . "

And we labor from youth to old age, convinced there's no alternative.

By the sweat of their brows shall ye know them.

But the open secret of ethnology is that the economy of "primitive" people before disruption by outside invasion almost always allowed for the satisfaction of their needs.

At the cost of a limited period of productive activity.

They were leisure societies, affluent societies.

Among the remaining Yanomami of Venezuela and Brazil, all needs of society are covered by three hours of work per person per day for adults.

"It is a civilization of leisure since they spend twenty-one hours doing nothing. They keep themselves amused. Siestas, practical jokes, arguments, drugs, eating, taking a dip, they manage to kill time. Not to mention sex."

Chronicles from the sixteenth and seventeenth centuries point to even less time spent working.

Actual labor clearing the land for crops sometimes involved no more than two months every other year.

Can such a life be measured in clock time?

From *Society Against the State* by Clastres—

"One cannot have it both ways: either man in primitive societies lives in a subsistence economy and spends most of his time in the search for food; or else he does not live in a subsistence economy and can allow himself prolonged hours of leisure, smoking in his hammock.

"That is what made an unambiguously unfavorable impression on the first European observers of the Indians of Brazil. Great was their disapproval on seeing that those strapping men glowing with health preferred to deck themselves out like women with paint and feathers instead of perspiring away in their gardens. Obviously these people were deliberately ignorant of the fact that one must earn his daily bread by the sweat of his brow.

"It wouldn't do, and it didn't last: the Indians were soon put to work, and they died of it. As a matter of fact, two axioms seem to have guided the advance of Western civilization from the outset: the first maintains that true societies unfold in the protective shadow of the State; the second states a categorical imperative: man must work."

Fifteenth-century chronicles are unanimous in describing the fine appearance of the adults, the good health of the many children, the abundance and variety of things to eat.

"The figures obtained, whether they concern nomad hunters of the Kalahari Desert or Amerindian sedentary agriculturalists, reveal a mean apportionment of less than four hours daily for ordinary work time. Thus we find ourselves at a far remove from the wretchedness that surrounds the idea of a subsistence economy.

"This means that primitive societies have at their disposal, if they so desire, all the time necessary to increase the production of material goods. Common sense asks then: why would the men living in those societies want to work and produce more? What good would it do them? Men work more than their needs require only when forced to. And it is just that kind of force which is absent from the primitive world."

And today, how long do our needs require us to work?
What determines those needs?
Have they been internalized from some unknown source?
What is the origin of our deepest convictions?

Does the metaphor of mind parasites upset you?

Remember that spooky afternoon in the elementary school auditorium?

(Don't be afraid. *Try to remember.*)

They called it a fire drill.

They called it a vaccination.

They called it lots of things.

Are we all being taken for a ride, and if so, by whom?

Today, those among us fortunate enough to be gainfully employed—that is, to have some money in the bank, a late-model car, medical insurance—work in excess of eight hours a day, with cell phones in our pockets and computers on our laps.

Not to mention the stressed-out commute to and fro.

Not to mention the anxious planning for a future which never quite arrives.

If the truth be told, maybe we never stop working.

But let's return to our exceptional sixteenth-century French teenager.

La Boétie intuited that "the society in which people want to serve the tyrant is historical, that it is not eternal and has not always existed, that it has a date of birth and that something must have happened . . . for men to fall from freedom into servitude."

(For a contemporary feel, substitute "corporation" for "tyrant.")

At the dawn of the sixteenth century, the first Europeans judged the Indians of South America as savages without faith, law, or king.

"Noting that chiefs held no power over the tribes, that one neither commanded nor obeyed, they declared that these people were not policed, that these were not veritable societies."

This is the key, dear reader—that chiefs held no power over their tribes.

La Boétie asked what misfortune so denatured people—born in truth to live freely—to make them lose the memory of their first existence and the desire to retrieve it.

"Misfortune: tragic accident, bad luck, the effects of which grow to the point of abolishing previous memory. What does La Boétie say? Clairvoyantly, he first affirms that this passage from freedom into servitude was unnecessary; he calls the division of society into those who command and those who obey accidental. What is designated here is indeed this moment of the birth of History, this fatal rupture which should never have happened, this irrational event which we moderns call the birth of the State.

"In society's fall into the voluntary submission of almost all people to a single person, La Boétie deciphers the abject sign of a perhaps irreversible decline: the new man is no longer a man, or even an animal, since 'animals cannot adapt to serving except with protest of a contrary desire . . .' Losing freedom, man loses his humanity. What misfortune indeed was able to bring him to renounce his being and make him desire the perpetuation of this renouncement?

"The sign and proof of this loss of freedom can be witnessed not only in the resignation to submission but in the love of servitude. The result of this split between free society and slave society is that all divided societies are slave societies. There is no good prince with whom to contrast the evil tyrant. What does it matter whether the prince is kind or cruel: whatever the case, is it not the prince whom people serve? There is no progressive slide from freedom to servitude . . . only the brutal misfortune which drowns the before of freedom in the after of submission.

"What does this mean? It means that all relationships of power are oppressive, that all divided societies are inhabited by absolute Evil, that society, as anti-nature, is the negation of freedom.

"The birth of History, the division between good and bad society are a result of misfortune: a good society is one in which the natural absence of division assures the reign of freedom, a bad society is one whose divided being allows the triumph of tyranny." (Pierre Clastres)

How about that, dear reader?

Makes you stop and think, doesn't it?

Listen to echoes down through the centuries—

Wild vs. domesticated, equals vs. caste, spirit vs. religion, community vs. private property, balanced whole vs. metastasizing part, raw vs. cooked.

Division is not an imperative of society.

"Before the unfortunate appearance of social division, there was necessarily, in conformity to man's nature, a society without oppression and without submission. Primitive societies are egalitarian: no one is worth more or less than another, no one is superior or inferior. In other words . . . no one is the holder of power.

"But once the misfortune has come to pass, once the freedom that naturally governed the relations between equals has been lost, absolute Evil is capable of anything: there is a hierarchy of the worst, and the totalitarian State . . . is there to remind us that however profound the loss of freedom, it is never lost enough, we never stop losing it.

"Desire for submission, refusal of obedience: society with a State, society without a State. Primitive societies refuse power relations by preventing the desire for submission from coming into being. As social machines inhabited by the will to persevere in their non-divided being, primitive societies institute themselves as places where evil desire is repressed.

"This desire has no chance: the Savages want nothing to do with it. The blossoming of the evil, two-faced desire which perhaps haunts all societies and all individuals of all societies must be prevented."

In every tribe Clastres studied, initiatory rites of the most extreme nature brought the adolescents who survived to a place of equal footing with adults.

Scars on their bodies serving as permanent reminders of equality.

"We see clearly now that it is not necessary to have had the experience of the State in order to refuse it . . . To its children the tribe proclaims: you are equal, no one among you is worth more than another, no one worth less than another, inequality is forbidden, for it is false, it is wrong." (Pierre Clastres)

These tribes are *purposefully* organized to deny the chief any opportunity for the exercise of what we call political power.

He is chosen for his oratorical talents, his generosity, his ability to resolve disputes, to bring peace to the community.

He has prestige but no personal power.

He is admired but not obeyed.

His will can't supercede that of the tribe.

In those rare instances when the chief desires to amass personal power—usually through scheming to take his tribe into a war it doesn't want—he is ignored.

If he insists, the others abandon or kill him.

In *Society Against the State*, Clastres points out the difference between this world and ours.

In our world of leaders and citizens, bosses and workers, masters and servants, power is detached from society as a whole since it's held by only a few members.

(And every little tinhorn mimics the structure—who's not acquainted with the bully in the schoolyard, the tyrant in the mail-room, the bad boy in the bedroom?)

The State apparatus—from ancient despotisms through totalitarian regimes to democratic societies—remains in remote control of legitimate violence.

(How our kiddies love their remote-control toys.)

It does this through the law.

Law imposing the power of the few on all others.

That is the king's law, the law of the State, "of which the Mandan and the Guaycurú, the Guayakí, and the Abipone know nothing.

"Whereas the law they come to know through initiation says: *You are worth no more than anyone else; you are worth no less than anyone else*. The law, inscribed on bodies, expresses primitive society's refusal to run the risk of division, the risk of a power separated from society itself, *a power that would escape its control.*"

Societies of the mark are societies without a State, societies against the State.

But the separate, distant, despotic law of the State is law that establishes and guarantees inequality.

"It is proof of their admirable depth of mind that the Savage knew all that *ahead of time*, and took care, at the cost of a terrible cruelty, to prevent the advent of a more terrifying cruelty: *the law written on the body is an unforgettable memory.*"

And the mark of our society, is it an invisible loss of memory?

But I can't possibly be proposing a return to the wild, can I?

Forget about it!

We ain't interested in life in the bush, picking the lice out of one another's hair, even if our faces would be wreathed in smiles.

We ain't interested in a diet of fruits and roots, with fat wriggling insect larvae for protein.

Indoor plumbing is cool, Mozart is cool, mayonnaise is cool.

Air conditioning is cool, two-way mirrors are cool, tiramisu is cool.

Palm Pilots are cool, Tylenol is cool, Limp Bizkit is cool.

Car alarms are cool, contact lenses are cool, Belgian waffles are cool.

Chemotherapy is cool, the Pentagon is cool, free airport luggage carts are cool.

Stiletto heels are cool, malathion is cool, duck à l'orange is cool.

Descartes is cool, Newton is cool, Galileo is cool.

Novartis is cool, Astro-Zeneca is cool, Cargill is cool.

Logo tattoos are cool, voiceprint IDs are cool, foie gras is cool.

Intellectual property rights are cool, metal detectors are cool, a nation of strangers is cool.

Wristwatches are cool, acid rain is cool, cellulite is cool.

Bikini burns are cool, Viagra is cool, Maalox is cool.

IQ tests are cool, the Ten Commandments are cool, Sigmund Freud is cool.

Vodka is cool, the Sistine Chapel is cool, Arby's is cool.

Dry cleaning is cool, collagen injections are cool, Mother Theresa is cool.

Tennis elbow is cool, Karl Marx is cool, peanut butter and jelly sandwiches are cool.

Prime time is cool, the Super Bowl is cool, edible vaccines are cool.

Polyester is cool, hospital hallways are cool, Olestra is cool.

Gatorade is cool, seedless watermelon is cool, multitracking is cool.

Side effects are cool, call waiting is cool, talking ATMs are cool.

Life insurance is cool, smart bombs are cool, drum machines are cool.

Waterproof mascara is cool, angel dust is cool, pollen drift is cool.

Clitoridectomies are cool, interferon is cool, Diet Coke is cool.

Income tax is cool, Tampax is cool, five thousand bonus miles are cool.

Skydiving is cool, tuxedos are cool, the pope is cool.

Sadism is cool, masochism is cool, french fries are cool.

Sèvres china is cool, Nazi memorabilia is cool, Saran wrap is cool.

Prenuptual agreements are cool, Pratesi sheets are cool, quid pro quo is cool.

Sound bites are cool, Pop-Tarts are cool, AZT is cool.

Viral loads are cool, road rage is cool, family values are cool.

Little League is cool, frozen embryos are cool, Ouchless Band-Aids are cool.

Holy Books are cool, holy wars are cool.

Survival of the fittest is cool, reasonable doubt is cool.

Zoloft is cool, Picasso is cool, KFC is cool.

Zoos are cool, planned obsolescence is cool.

Truffle-infused walnut oil is cool.

The last black rhinoceros on the planet is cool.

Contraceptive corn is cool.

Escaped transgenic salmon are cool.

Patented life forms are cool.

Cell phones are way cool.

We won't give up any of these things, so don't even ask.

Let's be realistic instead.

Let's concentrate on compromise solutions.

Let's all work together for a better world.

But don't go near my nest egg or I'll bite your fucking head off.

I may smile at you but I'll never turn my back on you because I don't trust you.

I do what I have to do to stay in business.

I make all the right moves to protect my investment.

And when things get gnarly my final hope lies in repression—the hired gun—no matter how many touchy-feely seminars I organize.

No matter how many church socials I attend.

No matter how many Insight Dialogue workshops I sign up for.

In fact, no matter how much I wish it to be otherwise.

That's just the way life is, dear reader.

It's all or nothing—I have all or I have nothing.

In American political terms, everyone's a Republican if pushed far enough.

The light of sharing goes out of our eyes.

The electric gates are installed, the metal detectors, the infrared sensors.

Gated communities proliferate where once there were family farms.

We remember the open space of our childhoods with nostalgia, and our parents and grandparents remember even more—the integrity of Mom and Pop farming their own land.

The decency of the old ways.

But look back far enough—ever since the appearance of herds and storehouses—you'll see less jarring, less extreme versions of the same thing.

Shit just took a while to reach this level.

The acceleration ferocious now, but it came on slowly, in unnoticed increments.

Generation after generation.

At most we're aware of its effects from one decade to the next.

Everything a blur now.

No time to pause anymore, there's too much to do.

One news item after another spells disaster but we can't focus—NAFTA's backwash, cheap American corn and sugar bankrupting fourteen percent more Mexican farmers each year.

Global temperature rises one degree in the past fifty years, nine degrees since the last Ice Age, but we look the other way.

The Pacific island nation of Tuvalu unnoticed as it's lost to rising waves.

The incidence of skin cancer in Greenland quadruples in twelve years but we turn the page.

In five years the planet stripped of its tropical flora over an area two and a half times the size of Italy.

U.S. wild honeybee population one-fourth of its former self.

The world's human population 6.1 billion in 2001, twice what it was in 1960.

Water use increasing six times in the past seventy years.

Species vanish like Kewpie dolls shot down at the county fair.

We giggle as cartoon animals take their place.

Forests clear-cut, topsoil washed away.

This realm of Mutually Assured Destruction.

This weed-strewn lot where daily portions of protein are rushed toward the stun gun.

Where ice chests filled with pharmaceuticals are handed out to the lucky ones.

Where everyone denies the sound of oil wells in the distance.

("I swear I don't hear anything, do you?")

A deep, metallic pounding.

Twenty-four hours a day, seven days a week, 365 days a year.

No mountain high enough, no ocean deep enough to escape from the sound.

Except by means of distraction.

Jack up the "music" till we can't hear ourselves think.

Vote for the background noise.

Ah, media, how we worship you.

Television angel of mercy.

Without your presence the grinding of the wells would long ago have driven us mad.

Acceleration's electric embrace.

How can we live without you?

Why would we even try?

In reality, citizen's initiatives are everywhere.

People taking back responsibility for their lives.

The power of citizen networking lies in its lack of defined structure.

Instead of one person leading while the rest simply follow.

Enabling these movements to surround and immobilize the most powerful institutions.

Organizing to save mangroves in the Ivory Coast, reef systems in Belize, wildlife in Namibia.

In China, India, Tasmania, Canada, Thailand, France, and Hungary, resisting dam projects that threaten homes and livelihoods.

Indigenous people leading the way—blockading logging roads in Malaysia with their own bodies.

Mobilizing in the Philippines to challenge destructive mining corporations.

Protecting rainforests of Ecuador from foreign oil companies.

Stopping government agribusiness from driving them off their farms.

But underneath corporate media's thick blue blanket, how much do we hear about these initiatives?

Around and around we go
When the plug's finally pulled
Escape velocity hurls us clear outside the trance
We sheer off into the bush
Bawling like babies
Completely at a loss

Outside the trance someone is waiting for us.

An old Indian man, five feet tall, wearing a cast-off T-shirt and torn shorts.

He sits on the ground tending a fire.

Around him assemble a dozen or so sick white people.

"Sick" meaning sick with civilization, though many also are burdened by specific physical ailments.

All have come here to be healed, though they're also uneasy.

Everything they've heard about ayahuasca has led them to expect an experience bursting with revelations, spectacular visions—and naked fear.

For days now, mosquitoes have been feasting on their skin.

The food has been starchy and bland, the water suspect.

They've been challenged by the humid heat and strange surroundings.

At dusk it seems to get dark instantaneously.

The resonating insects in the blackness of the forest are multilayered and very loud.

Larger sounds of animals or birds punctuate the din.

The white people feel their "who I am"s melting.

And all this before they take even one sip of the fabled brew.

La Purga—the purge—it's called down here in the jungle.

The old man's smile is gentle and sweet but he seems preoccupied. He's singing to himself, already half in another world.

The tour leader who brought them here from Quito in the mountains reassures everyone that what's coming will transform them.

"It'll change your lives," he rhapsodizes. "Your hearts will open, you'll connect with everyone here, make friends for life. You'll return to the States with new priorities. You'll be an inspiration to your friends and loved ones. You'll help save this planet. Cynicism and defeat banished forever."

They believe him—they like him—they even trust him, but he's not drinking, he informs them.

"Someone's gotta stay on the ground," he says. "I'll be right here if you need me."

Need him for what, they wonder nervously.

But in spite of second thoughts they're eager for this adventure, they're determined to follow through, every last one of them. They've been told about ayahuasca from friends. They signed on willingly.

The curandero motions for everyone to sit down.

An ancient Indian woman materializes out of the shadows behind him. Her features are unreadable in the gloom but her presence is reassuring. Her wraithlike essence seems to float through everyone as she blows tobacco smoke into one face after another and strokes perspiring bodies with a fan made of fresh leaves.

"*O, virgen del sol*," the old man sings in Spanish.

He begins whispering in a herky-jerky rhythm which bounces back and forth in the air like a little sprite.

"*Mi corazón*," he sings.

Then he's singing in some other language as he lifts the lid from a battered metal pot and beckons to the person sitting closest to him.

The brew tastes bitter, foul even.

One after another the voyagers gag it down.

"Relax," the guide says. "Don't resist. Don't be afraid."

"Heal me Momma," a voice erupts in English. "Heal me."

The words sound unexpectedly poignant, and even before the brew takes hold several people are weeping.

Then the air crackles, the atmosphere changes.

A presence approaches from afar.

At first things seem almost the same as before.

Then suddenly something tremendously powerful is right on top of everyone, tearing away at them, blowing them to pieces.

Finally their egos dissolve in bursts of light and streams of unbearably intense images.

Grimacing semi-human faces, huge twisting snakes, gorgeously colored embodiments of self-mockery and of exaltation.

All this piles into quaking psyches with the force of a tidal wave.

Nowhere to run, nowhere to hide.

Finally egos dissolve . . .

But maybe I'm kidding myself.

How many people would remain smug and judgmental after such an experience?

Is there a clear-cut divide in the human race?

A perceptual split screen?

On one side are those unaffected by the drone of the killer machinery.

They willingly give themselves over to it.

While we others, we sensitive plants, tremble and grow heartsick.

(The poet William Carlos Williams, 1955, opening the curtains in his living room. Pointing at the street, he confides to his visitors, "There are a lot of bastards out there.")

Consequences mean nothing to them.

Satan's not some quaint Biblical figure.

Satan is another way of saying I don't care.

His eyes filled with mock concern as he grinds his boot heel in your face.

Satan gets up earlier than the rest of the angels, eager to cheat, to torture.

Satan is without conscience.

"Blood is a very special juice," he says.

He laughs while selling out-of-date drugs, banned pesticides.

He steals land from trusting farmers and murders those who protest.

He develops a strategy for global hegemony and calls it progress.

Always he makes his presence known by an unremitting noise.

Loudspeakers in every public place, transmitters humming on rooftops, snowmobiles crashing through the wilderness.

Drowning out the competition, sucking up all personal space.

Everything he touches turns into poison.

Sugarcane turns into slavery, coca leaves into crack cocaine, tobacco the universal offering to plant spirits turns into cancer sticks, paralytic smoke inhaled by millions.

Satan the motherfucker, pounding his drill bit deep into the Mother, submerging clean energy alternatives in an avalanche of propaganda.

Satan is unrestrained ego, standardizing all of life out of fear.

Ego's fantasy of control in perpetuity.

Blind to the consequences of its own actions.

Insatiable ego, rampaging without cease.

Corrupt and oblivious, lightning-quick, always one step ahead because never hesitating.

Always ready with the plausible explanation, the reasonable excuse.

Ego nimble and devious.

Ego two-faced, fork-tongued.

Ego eyes in the back of its head, ego fingers in every pie, indomitable and tireless, never resting, never doubting, never letting down its guard.

Ego not me first but just me—only me, nothing but me from beginning to end.

From the first moment of separation to the last gasp of existence.

Always uneasy, unsatisfied, petulant.

Always on guard, always ready to betray.

Always aggrieved, plotting how to strike back, get even.

Paranoid and full of rage, seeing enemies everywhere.

(O Saddam Hussein, with your official tasters, your obsession with germs, your killer's glance striking panic in all who cross your path. You're one among many, Saddam, a figure recurring over and over in recorded history—the pitiless tyrant. But does that make your outbursts of treachery and slaughter any less monstrous?)

Ego making solid what actually is transparent.

Ego defending an illusion with murderous finality.

An illusion mutually reinforced by cultural mindsets installed for millennia.

Everybody's doin' it, how can we possibly refrain?

Without nuclear deterrents we're sitting ducks.

If we don't churn out more warheads we're victims, naked and effeminate.

"They'll take advantage of us, they'll rush in and annihilate us."

Annals of warfare in the Bible. Ancient accounts of Hittites, Greeks, Aryans, Chinese.

Always the same justification, the same explanation: if not them, us. So them before us.

But they are us.

No difference between bloodthirsty enemies, between Palestinians and Jews, between communists and capitalists, between guerrillas and paramilitaries.

Ego's identifications and projections instantaneous, worldwide, self-fulfilling.

We/they locked in identical vision.

Looking outside we see life but it's really a mirror.

We see difference but it's just repetition.
Treacherous virus eternally poised for invasion.

But maybe I'm too enraged to see clearly.
Time to take my own advice and breathe.
In and out. In and out. Slowly.
Letting go of all thoughts as they arise.
Because deep inside I know beliefs create experience.
My reality nothing other than my beliefs.
Magnified by the millions, just like a magic trick, the reality of a
nation appears.
Reality of a region, a hemisphere, the globe.
No wonder beliefs are defended with such ferocity.
Every last one of them is arbitrary!

If so, why not remain upbeat?
Then the last eight thousand years become nothing more than a
birthing period, a learning stage.
Chrysalis for the new human.
Well worth the wait.
(*The new human*—after all, both New Age dreamers and the new
eugenicists are convinced we're molting big time. The question is,
into what?)
As with the Bomb, maybe we'll proceed to the brink of destruc-
tion then save ourselves.
Degraded lives, trashed environment—the price to pay for trans-
formation?
Holy paradigm shift! Sacred singularity! Age of Aquarius!
Because human ingenuity always saves the day.
You can bet that after the oil wells run dry, grain alcohol or solar
energy or fuel cells will take their place.
Sooner or later, in fact, the internal combustion engine will be a
museum piece, replaced by something of which at present we can't
conceive.

A sabem woirjabke cuvuc gkibakuzatuib wukk taje tge okace if ecibinuc gkao—beating our heads against the wall trying to decipher what remains utter gibberish until the right moment, when suddenly—

A sane, workable, civil globalization takes the place of economic globalization.

A new planetary civilization without the old ethnic and class animosities.

Former headhunters leading junketeers into the rainforest to identify colorful wildlife.

Former guerrillas, extortionists, and kidnappers dancing in folk costume on picturesque village squares.

Former secret-police operatives weaving baskets on dirt floors for their new extended families.

Former caudillos emptying bedpans in old age homes.

Vision of universal inclusiveness!

A future where wealth is shared.

Where everyone has enough to eat, free medical care, safe water, a decent place to live.

Peace on Earth! The lion lies down with the lamb!

Fantasyland, you say?

But that dream of arrival, of return to the Garden, has been with us ever since the Old Taskmaster threw us out.

He must have known what he was doing.

Because when he booted us out—for the crime of knowing what we had, what by rights was ours—he sentenced man to eternal labor.

He sentenced woman to perpetual submission and the pain of childbirth.

He outlawed pleasure.

In other words, he was a stand-in for the ruling classes.

But what if no ruling classes remain, so there's nothing left to defend?

If ragged bands of Indians wandering the jungle can do it, why can't we?

What if money turns into confetti?

What if no diseases survive—no doctors and pharmaceuticals,

no hospitals and medical insurance—because everyone eats raw plant food?

What if sexuality becomes a walk in the park, a return to the discoveries of childhood?

What if highways and strip malls, tenements and skyscrapers are recycled, like so much cardboard, into open space?

What if the dream of inclusion becomes reality, the uncovering of a tribal seed we've all buried somewhere and lost track of these many centuries, searching for it in religious cults, in therapy, in political parties, stadium sports, groups and alliances of all kinds?

What if hyperscience drops its load of invasive toys into a black hole of simple presence?

What if intuition and vision replace cell phones and computer virus codes?

What if monocultures of the mind give way to an embrace of biodiversity?

Agribusiness just a sour dream.

Genetic intervention a misshapen chimera flushed down the toilet of time.

7.

Because not all who wander are lost.

Today, as never before, we have the chance to start over.

How fortunate we are to live in the end times!

Every belief called into question, every sacred cow demystified, every tradition decaying.

But only if we step outside our mental houses.

Only if we embrace the unknown.

Then psychotropic substances—to cite one path among many— can facilitate a new life.

A life unburdened even by beliefs of the jungle Indians themselves, many of which are hardly empowering.

The last thing we need, to exchange hidebound rationalism for the claustrophobic sorcery of Amazonia.

Instead of romanticizing archaic cultures, we find our own way.

Held hostage by no one's past, not even our own.

"The evil eye, envy and fear are not generally recognized as causes of disease in Western medicine. We do not easily believe in such diagnoses and usually label them as naïve superstitions. Yet, shamans routinely cure individuals who are genuinely physically ill by working within this frame of reference. This is psychosomatic medicine, pure and simple, and seems to have more to do with psychiatry than 'general practice'—or does it? Where do you draw the line between mind and matter?

"Belief per se seems to have a certain potency of its own. In other words, if enough energy is given to a belief it may be possible for it to become a force of nature able to employ other, more generic forces in its service.

"The concept of 'hypothesis' comes to mind: Ideally, a working hypothesis has built within it a potential for modification, even continuous modification. Beliefs, on the other hand, tend to be problematic precisely because they are usually fixed and resistant to self-correction. An hypothesis assumes that we don't know but are trying to learn. A belief insists on the comforting illusions of certitude."
(*Psychedelic Shamanism*, Jim DeKorne)

The stakes of the game being played—
Just who do we think we are?
Once we step outside of ego's bomb shelter, no belief is solid.
Consensus reality becomes transparent.
Beliefs—nests and layers and sets of them, beliefs inside beliefs, echoing and surrounding us, anticipating our every move.
Beliefs handed down through generations, beliefs inserted in our mindstreams at birth, beliefs reinforced by education and media.
Beliefs we take home to meet the folks.
Beliefs we sit down and eat for dinner.
Indoctrination into the status quo.
Norms of collective resignation.
But whatever's done can be undone—
How amazing that nature wants us to survive!
She wants us to be free.
She manifests antidotes even when we ignore her.
She gives us plant spirits to lift us out of trance.
So we can watch ourselves from outside the creation within which we've been enfolded.
And start a new life.

What form might that life take?
Dismantling the demon involves some unsexy choices.
Living simply.

Sustaining instead of devouring.

"Think globally, act locally."

How this slogan exasperates us!

Do you really expect me to trade in my Lexus for a bicycle?

Give up awesome stadium blowouts to sit around a campfire telling stories?

(What stories would I tell?)

Walk away from my state-of-the-art electronic interfaces?

Kill my television?

Give me a break!

But hold on a second—maybe rejecting technology only amounts to thinking along the same old adversarial axis.

The real paradigm shift not going backward or forward but out.

Not future versus past but openness instead of constriction.

A free fall through infinitely collapsing beliefs.

And once this cumbersome, inert, mechano-chemical structure grinds to a halt, then what?

Can globalization be a positive force, an integration with planetary and galactic destiny?

How are we to interpret the Mayan calendar's prediction for the year 2012?

World upheaval meaning obliteration or transformation, disaster or opportunity.

Depending on our point of view.

Definition of human—we're more than our names in the phone book.

"The twenty-first century will be spiritual or it won't be at all." (André Malraux)

The twenty-first century will be communal or it won't be at all.

But some of us can't wait, we want it all now.

In the far reaches of ego's space the longing for connection can be irresistible.

Lonely ego encased in its rocket ship, aimed like a finger at the distant cold stars.

We'd give anything to drop the game of separateness we're forced to play.

Give anything to merge, to look other people in the eye with unguarded affection.

Puppies in a big warm pile, licking and sniffing and whimpering.

Swooning into the arms of whoever's standing next to you.

Without hesitation your heart melts, its golden nectar flowing to whoever you're with at the moment.

The warmth you feel for that person what you'd feel for your oldest, dearest friend.

That person's eyes become your lover's eyes.

"We're all brothers and sisters. We're all in this together."

Unconditional receptivity for someone you've never met before.

Torrid embraces with total strangers.

Strangers?

The term loses meaning in the rave culture.

The term loses meaning when you take Ecstasy with thousands of others, jammed together in an old warehouse or airplane hangar, the world outside banished for days on end.

Have you ever tried Ecstasy, dear reader?

Strong medicine.

Body, mind, and spirit become trusting, joyous, open.

You're dancing nonstop.

Your skin's on fire, you're dying to be touched, caressed.

Your teeth gritting, your eyeballs skittering—physical reactions involuntary, excessive, so what?

You're eighteen, twenty, twenty-three years old.

You call up an ancient, vanished tribe still present somewhere deep in your bones.

Never mind that you need a synthetic chemical to open up and connect.

Never mind the stories of damage done over time—the myelin sheath of your nerves worn away, the memory impairment.

Ah, memory, a mixed blessing!

Who cares how much we forget of this killer culture?

In fact, the more the better.

In fact, everybody's memory is in decline.

Let the computers remember for us, isn't that their purpose anyway?

At least we get to embrace our fellow humans wholeheartedly.

At least we get to taste the dewdrops of the Golden Age, still sparkling and clear and fresh.

Because it's a mistake to think this culture will last much longer.

Walking on eggshells, out on a limb, state of denial.

Western white noise powered by psychotic episodes dressed up as healthy ambition.

Western white noise, how I long to hear the silence behind your posturing.

But, unlike me, nature's not impatient.

She waits, compassionate, all-knowing.

Time means nothing to her.

She doesn't care if a million years go by before life's balance is restored.

She laughs—you can't hear her laugh but it's everywhere, in the crowding and acceleration, in the epidemics and famines, in the ruined lives—she laughs at the desperate compulsions spewing out of Western white noise's mouth.

She laughs at the very disasters which are destroying her.

Yes, even my clairvoyant glimpses of revenge, of oil industry meltdown, she views with a trickster gleam in her eye, indifferent to any outcome.

She smiles at those working tirelessly for her benefit because she knows their egos are involved in what they say and do.

Whereas her power is beyond ego, beyond name and form, beyond individual identity, beyond striving.

The great detachment of the Goddess, breathtaking and fearful.

The terrible distance from which she churns out and ingests all life—good and bad, beautiful and ugly, vital and sickly, just and monstrous.

The indifference of the stars, the galaxies which come and go without explanation, without bias, without a sound.

The silence of the Goddess making any witness—even the bravest of all—crumple in awe, "go blind in her presence," as the ancient texts averred.

Because she doesn't care the way "you" and "I" care.

No matter how bad things get, she knows her survival is beyond influence.

No matter the polar ice caps melt, no matter the half-life of nuclear stockpiles leaking into everyone's tomorrow, no matter the disappearance of her precious creatures, her trees and flowers, no matter the poisoning of her air and water, no matter the end times.

End times for us is nothing to her, literally nothing at all.

Looking us in the eye—her glance that burns our retinas—she reaches under her gown and fingers herself, making herself wet, making herself come, over and over again.

Out of her moaning mouth spill unending life-forms, forever taking the place of what disappears.

That's all she does, from here to eternity.

And we can't believe it, we refuse to accept it, the knowledge of our insignificance pulverizes us.

Going blind in her presence—isn't that what we're doing right now?

How long has it been since we've seen the world with any semblance of accuracy?

How long since our infantile withdrawal into technology, locking us into a Dark Age beyond compare because briskly paced and brightly lit?

"Immaturity is the most effective term to define our contemporaries . . . An immature state which a *culture that has become inorganic* creates and releases within us." (Witold Gombrowicz)

Deaf and dumb infants of techno-crisis, blind to the daylight we've beaten out of the rest of humanity.

How else to explain the willful destruction of our planet but by a triumph of infantile projection?

"Might not the acknowledged disturbance of the maturation process, with its intellectual, sexual, affective and psycho-motor disorders, and the immaturity of individuals who remain arrested in childhood, be the logical outcome and final manifestation of technological defects which have become hereditary?

"Without even suspecting it, we have become the heirs and descendants of some fearsome antecedents, the prisoners of hereditary defects transmitted now not through the genes, sperm or blood but through *an unutterable technical contamination.*

"By virtue of this loss of 'behavioral freedom,' all criticism of technology has just about disappeared and we have slid unconsciously from pure technology to techno-culture and, lastly, to the dogmatism of a *totalitarian techno-cult* in which everyone is caught in the trap . . . of what these centuries of progress have made of us and *of our own bodies.*"

(*The Information Bomb*, Paul Virilio)

Faster, smaller, cheaper—doesn't that describe not simply the devices we use but who we are?

Corporate globalization the leading edge of this juggernaut, while at every turn suspicion reinforces our disconnect.

We take refuge in litigation at the first sign of disagreement.

We bolt the door and turn out the lights.

You don't know me at all.

I who am your neighbor, your lover, your friend.

"Don't touch me. Don't come near me, stranger. Don't invade my space."

Faster, smaller, cheaper—our geography mimicking the orbit within which we live.

And the microbiologists, heroes of the moment, manipulating life at an invisible level where nothing's certain.

Yet it's there we look for deliverance, dredging up monsters from the deep.

People alike in every respect except for the quaint, distinctive details which keep us from waking up psychopathic.

Which keep us from discovering the trick, the game, the payoff.

The trick of predictability.

The game of submission.

The payoff of control.

Tele-surveillance.

Not simply cameras watching you in public places—that's just for show, for the delinquents and hotheads, loose cannons factored into society's equation to lend it spice, believability.

Tele-surveillance means that if you and I and everyone else watch the same things on television and at the movies, read the same books and magazines, go to the same places, we're echoes or variations of the same person.

As alike as the hairs on an arm.

Except that the original's missing.

Because for purposes of control no original is needed.

Musically we've become a field of reverbs.

Tribal call and response with the original call edited out.

Interpenetrations of absence.

Tele-surveillance isn't simply restricted to orbiting satellites, to the hardware which keeps track of us.

Tele-surveillance applies equally to the software installed within.

It's our expectations, the limits we accept, our comfort zone, our inability to conceive of another way of life.

The drop-off into self-doubt at the cliff's edge.

Tele-surveillance means never having to worry that the people will rise up in revolt, because revolution is outmoded, something occurring in history books, in flickering images from last century's newsreels.

Tele-surveillance, the apple of Mother's eye.

"Don't stray too far, dear. You never know what's out there. Stay under the light of the street lamps. Stay within range of my cell phone. Stay put. Stay your hand."

This not the voice of the Goddess but of her inverse, her usurper.

The Usurper is whoever tells you you can't, you shouldn't, you won't.

Whoever watches intently, never relaxing for a moment the gaze which restricts you.

Superego carping and criticizing, cutting you off from your life force.

Tele-surveillance locked into standardization itself.

Trouble-free. No surprises.

". . . the full-scale over-exposure not just of places—as with the remote surveillance of roads—but also of persons, their behavior, their actions and innermost reactions.

"Thus the misleading nature of enforced competition becomes a part of our economic, political and cultural activities.

"The multinational enterprise sidelines the weak at their key-pads; it sidelines these new 'citizens of the world' as mere consumers of a kind of *parlor game* in which the conditioned reflex wins out over shared reflection.

"After ordinary 'grassing,' calumny and slander . . . we are now entering the era of *optical snooping.* This is bringing a general spread of surveillance cameras, not just into the streets, avenues, banks or supermarkets, but also into the home . . . with the worldwide prolif-eration of 'live-cams' on the Internet, where you can visit the planet from your armchair thanks to Earthcam, a server which already has 172 cameras sited in twenty-five countries. Or, alternatively, you can have access through Netscape Eye to thousands of on-line cameras angled not just at tourism and business but towards a generalized introspection.

"These are emblematic of a universal voyeurism which directs everyone's gaze towards privileged 'points of view,' the sudden increase in 'points of view' never being any other than a heralding of the future 'points of sale' of the latest globalization: *the globalization of the gaze of the single eye.*" (Paul Virilio)

Tele-surveillance going beyond tele, beyond surveillance.

Going right up against who we take ourselves to be.

Smaller, faster, cheaper.

So who do we take ourselves to be?

We view our system of knowledge as universal.

But the dominant system isn't universal.

Our knowledge emerged with the rise of commercial capitalism.
Our culture's favorite beliefs mirror the social projects of its creators.

Half the money the world spends on advertising goes to ten conglomerates producing everything that's seen, heard, and read.

In the year 2000, the average American viewed twenty-five thousand commercials.

"It is not necessary that the mass media create a genuine desire
for a consumerist way of life: all they have to do is prevent genuine
desire for any other way of life from being publicly expressed and
collectively affirmed." (Duane Elgin)

White noise drowning out all other sounds.

Who's that knocking at my door?

Who dares disrupt my peace?

The peace of outer space.

Perfect and trouble-free.

Monocultures of the Mind, Vandana Shiva—

"The universal/local dichotomy is misplaced when applied to
Western and indigenous traditions of knowledge, because the Western
is a local tradition which has been spread world-wide through intellectual colonization.

"The universal would spread in openness. The globalizing local
spreads by violence and misrepresentation. The first level of violence
unleashed on local systems of knowledge is to not see them as
knowledge. Local knowledge . . . is made to disappear by denying it
the status of a systematic knowledge and assigning it the adjectives
'primitive' and 'unscientific.' Correspondingly, the Western system is
assumed to be uniquely 'scientific' and universal. The prefix 'scientific' for the modern systems . . . has, however, less to do with knowledge and more to do with power.

"Over and above rendering local knowledge invisible by declaring it non-existent or illegitimate, the dominant system also makes
alternatives disappear by erasing and destroying the reality which
they attempt to represent.

"When the West colonized Asia, it colonized her forests. It

brought with it the ideas of nature and culture as derived from the model of the industrial factory. The forest was no longer viewed as having a value itself, in all its diversity.

"Tropical people also become a dispensable and historical waste. In place of cultural and biological pluralism, the factory produces non-sustainable monocultures in nature and society. The diversity must be weeded out and uniform monocultures—of plants and people—must now be externally managed because they are no longer self-regulated and self-governed. Those that do not fit into the uniformity must be declared unfit. Symbiosis must give way to competition, domination and dispensability. There is no survival possible for the forest or its people when they become feedstock for industry."

Watch how swiftly the dominator culture overturns traditional ways, dear reader.

Listen to the first foreigner accepted to make her home in India's isolated Himalayan region of Ladakh.

In 1975, Ladakh was opened to foreign tourists and "development" began in earnest.

Based on two decades of close contact with the people and her ability to speak the language, Helena Norberg-Hodge was able to observe the effect of these changes on the Ladakhis' perception of themselves—

"Within the space of little more than a decade, feelings of pride gave way to what can best be described as a cultural inferiority complex. In the modern sector today, most young Ladakhis are ashamed of their cultural roots and desperate to appear modern.

"When tourism first began in Ladakh, it was as though people from another planet suddenly descended on the region.

"Each day many tourists would spend as much as $100—an amount roughly equivalent to someone spending $50,000 per day in America. In the traditional subsistence economy, money played a minor role. Basic needs—food, clothing, and shelter—were provided for without money. The labor one needed was free of charge, part of an intricate web of human relationships.

"Ladakhis did not realize that money meant something very different for the foreigners, that back home they needed it to survive, that food, clothing, and shelter all cost money—a lot of money. Compared to these strangers, Ladakhis suddenly felt poor.

"This new attitude contrasted dramatically with the Ladakhis' earlier self-confidence. In 1975, I was shown around the remote village of Hemis Shukpachan by a young Ladakhi named Tsewang. It seemed to me that all the houses were especially large and beautiful. I asked Tsewang to show me the houses where the poor people lived. He looked perplexed a moment, then responded, 'We don't have any poor people.'

"Eight years later I overheard Tsewang talking to some tourists. 'If you could only help us Ladakhis,' he was saying, 'we're so poor.'

"Development has brought not only tourism but also Western and Indian films and, more recently, television. Together they provide overwhelming images of luxury and power. There are countless tools, magical gadgets, and machines—machines to take pictures, machines to tell time, machines to make fire, to travel from one place to another, to talk with someone far away. Machines can do everything; it's no wonder the tourists look so clean and have such soft, white hands.

"For young Ladakhis, the picture is irresistible. It is an overwhelmingly exciting version of an urban American Dream, with an emphasis on speed, youthfulness, super-cleanliness, beauty, fashion, and competitiveness.

"In contrast to these utopian images from another culture, village life seems primitive, silly, and inefficient. The one-dimensional view of modern life becomes a slap in the face.

"This is not surprising: looking as they do from the outside, all young Ladakhis can see is the material side of the modern world—the side in which Western culture excels. They cannot so readily see the social or psychological dimensions: the stress, the loneliness, the fear of growing old. Nor can they see the environmental decay, inflation, or unemployment. They rush after sunglasses, walkmans, and blue jeans—not because they find those jeans more attractive or comfortable but because they are symbols of modern life.

"I have seen people proudly wear wristwatches they cannot read and for which they have no use. Even the traditional foods are no longer a source of pride. Now when I'm a guest in a village, people apologize if they serve the traditional roasted barley, *ngamphe*, instead of instant noodles.

"A gap is developing between young and old, male and female, rich and poor, Buddhist and Muslim. Competition for jobs and political representation within the new centralized structures is increasingly dividing Ladakhis. Ethnic and religious differences have taken on a political dimension, causing bitterness and envy on a scale hitherto unknown.

"Having seen my friends change so dramatically, I have no doubt that the bonds and responsibilities of the traditional society, far from being a burden, offered a profound sense of security, which seems to be a prerequisite for inner peace and contentment. I am convinced people were significantly happier before development and globalization than they are today. The people were cared for, and the environment was well sustained—which criteria for judging a society could be more important?"

("The Pressure to Modernize and Globalize," Helena Norberg-Hodge, in *The Case Against the Global Economy*)

As in villages of Ladakh, so also in Nepal and Indonesia, Nigeria and Peru.

As in forests of India, so also in Central and South America, Africa and Asia.

As in pastureland of Australia and North America, so also in Central and South America.

As in workshops and ateliers of Asia and Africa, so also in Central and South America, North America and Europe.

Not resting till everyone on the planet has the same answer to the question, "What time is it?"

Because the Devil is standardization.

Out of fear he suppresses diversity.

One size fits all.

The automobiles we ride in identical except for the absence or presence of luxury detailing.

Lowest common denominator of style and performance, universal in its application.

Computers, furniture, clothing, food, vacations, language, music, art, people—everything modular.

World of interchangeable parts.

Planetary urbanite, ransoming your future for a clean, well-lighted, noisy place.

Fucking in unison, fighting in unison, moping around in unison.

Restricting yourself to irony and caustic fretfulness, to diminished expectations, to the motorized wheelchair of your security arrangements, your insurance records and contracts and guarantees.

And for all that, in your deepest dreams, never losing your desire for a swan dive into the unknown.

"Ten days without your keys, without your driver's license, without money. Pristine beaches, profusion of wildlife, roaming all afternoon and dancing all night. Ten days in Paradise."

But why only ten days?

As Bob Dylan sang thirty-five years ago, "Look out, kid, they keep it all hid."

And what happened to Bob? Did he become a real-estate mogul in spite of himself?

Because in the Usurper's world you either starve or break the bank.

In the Usurper's world everybody buys into the same game.

In the Usurper's world we feed the open mouth of sameness, gaping hole never filled.

Standardization going beyond death because it's death in life.

But—as we've seen—death in life is recent.

The Usurper is recent.

Sameness is recent.

Control is recent.

Recent meaning here since "recorded history" began.

The great empires of the ancient world were cruel and despotic.

Don't be fooled by their temples and monuments.

Don't be fooled by the grandeur of their pageants.

Don't be fooled by the regal beauty of their kings and queens.

From neolithic storehouses filled with grain to mafia suitcases stuffed with cash is one simple step.

But always hidden, always disguised.

Until the triumph of rationalism, that is.

Until the appearance of factories and assembly lines, until humans became cogs in a moneymaking machine.

Until efficiency experts and time-motion studies, until workers spied upon, until rosy futures mapped out for all.

Because fascism is more than a twentieth-century political movement.

It occurs whenever difference is neutralized.

It's the bundle of sticks all lined up in one direction, then tightly bound together.

Regardless of whether achieved by means of myths, physical intimidation, or modern advertising.

One coordinated step.

One goose step.

One lockstep.

In an age of amnesia, corporate globalization's buttery agenda of sameness wants us stoned.

Because we're all more or less alike when we're stoned.

Stoned with our paychecks in hand, stoned on our after-hours barstools, stoned on our reefer and powders and pills, stoned in our easy chairs in front of TV, stoned at our standard-issue entertainments, stoned behind the curtains of our lonely voting booths.

8.

Now's the time of the motherfuckers, when we try to shoot the Goddess in the heart.

The U'wa Indians of Colombia threaten mass suicide (October, 1997) if Occidental Petroleum continues to desecrate their ancestral lands.

They insist that the oil wells drain the blood of Mother Earth.

Dare we contradict them?

Now's the time of the motherfuckers.

Oil reserves in all of Ecuador projected to last for a mere twenty years.

When the drilling's over, the total amount will equal ten days' worth of U.S. gasoline consumption.

That's ten days of us riding around in circles from sea to shining sea, complaining about our stretch marks.

For this the Ecuadorian rainforest is decimated.

For this indigenous people's lives are deleted.

Now's the time of the motherfuckers, with pharmaceutical industry lackies sent into the Amazon to strip the Indians of their plant lore.

Now's the time of the motherfuckers, with subversion of the Kyoto Treaty's attempt to address a culture in which fossil fuels are burned with abandon.

Burning like a bonfire in tinder-dry woods.

Burning like the end times.

Madness of intoxication, beyond limits, beyond compunction.

Something inside us not wanting to stop.

Now's the time of the motherfuckers, men who form shadowy alliances inside shadowy alliances.

Drifting skeins of cash-driven power wrapped around the world, trying to turn the Goddess into a desiccated mummy.

Now's the time of the motherfuckers, April in Paris for squads of short necks in rancid leisure wear who sail their cruise ships right into Notre Dame cathedral.

"We're the final version of the Son of God, Mother Mary," they cry out in unison.

Now's the time of the motherfuckers, with uncounted millions of Chinese in medical and economic free fall, sacrificial victims of market logic.

Their inaccessible leaders living in walled compounds, just like emperors of old.

Just like billionaires in London, Moscow, and Palm Springs.

Don't let different cultural markers fool you.

Don't let the heat of competing nationalisms mislead you.

Underneath them all—China, France, Brazil, U.S.A.—the same ordering principle, market-driven and rationalist.

Whether controlled by corporate empires or corporate governments.

Whether dancing to the tune of dictators or democrats.

Whether indulging in border skirmishes or Star Wars.

Now's the time of the motherfuckers, good old boys building maquiladoras on the Mexican border where single mothers work for a dollar a day.

Now's the time of the motherfuckers, with American schoolchildren learning their numbers by counting Tootsie Rolls and Cheerios, and environmental safety by watching Exxon films.

Now's the time of the motherfuckers, brittle fashion plates choking down sickly Thanksgiving turkeys raised in cages the size of shoeboxes.

Then looking in the mirror and resolving to go for the liposuction.

Resolving to go organic, in hopes it'll help them live forever.

Now's the time of upper-middle-class motherfuckers, happy as clams, secure as dodo birds.

Now's the time of nuclear family motherfuckers, whose secret weapon is their love for their children.

In the name of that love they commit atrocities without thinking twice.

"I did it for the kids . . ."

In the name of that love they turn gold into lead, earth into dust, wood into ashes, water into carbolic acid.

In the name of that love they set fire to their own houses.

They break the bank, stab their best friends in the back.

In the name of that love, betrayal becomes necessity.

In a world of ceaseless competition, triumph over others the only option.

And so, dear one, what about accountability?

Who's responsible for this pirate raid we call Western civilization?

No one in particular.

According to the legal definition of a corporation, no one is responsible for its actions because the corporation itself is defined as a fictitious person.

It's defined as no one in particular.

Bhopal, Exxon Valdez, Love Canal, Times Beach.

Who's to blame?

No one in particular.

The corporate imperative ensnares all players.

CEOs of Union Carbide and Exxon genuinely grieving the day after disasters in India and Alaska.

Two weeks later, they take refuge in damage control and cover-ups.

Who's responsible?

Corporations are demons, nonpersons given personhood—

"That murder charges are not levied against corporations, and that corporations do not express shame at their own actions, is a direct result of the peculiar nature of the corporate form, its split personality. Though human beings work inside corporations, a corporation itself is not a person (except in the legal sense) and does not have feelings. A corporation is not even a thing. It may have offices and/or a factory where it may manufacture products, but a corporation does not have any physical existence or form—no *corporality*. So when conditions in a community or country become unfavorable it can dematerialize and rematerialize in another town or country.

"If a corporation is not a person or thing, what is it? It is basically a *concept* that is given a name and a legal existence on paper. Though there is no such actual creature, our laws recognize the corporation as an entity. So does the population. We think of corporations as having concrete form, but their true existence is only on paper and in our minds.

"Even more curious is the way our laws give this nonexistent entity a great many rights similar to those of human beings. The law calls corporations *fictitious persons*, with the right to buy and sell property or to sue in court for injuries, slander and libel. And *corporate speech*—advertising, public relations—is protected under the First Amendment to the Constitution governing freedom of speech.

"Though corporations enjoy many 'human rights,' they have not been required to abide by human responsibilities. Even in cases of negligence causing death or injury, the state cannot jail or execute a corporation. A corporation may be fined or ordered to alter its practices, but its structure is never altered—its 'life' is never threatened. Unlike human beings, corporations do not die a natural death."

("The Rules of Corporate Behavior," Jerry Mander, in *The Case Against the Global Economy*)

The peculiar nature of the corporate form, its split personality.

If corporations refuse to be held accountable for their actions, can they at least be judged schizophrenic and dealt with accordingly?

Where's the asylum for insane institutions?

Actually, it's in your state capitol, dear reader.

Because corporations and the rules under which they operate are based on state charters of incorporation.

And these charters can be amended.

"For one hundred years after the American Revolution, citizens and legislators fashioned the nation's economy by directing the chartering process.

"Having thrown off English rule and transformed corporate governments into constitutionalized states, the revolutionaries did not give governors, judges, or generals the authority to charter corporations. Citizens made certain that elected legislators issued charters, one at a time and for a limited number of years. They kept a tight hold on corporations by spelling out the rules each had to follow, by holding corporate managers, directors, and stockholders liable for harm or injuries, and by revoking charters.

"Because of widespread public involvement, early legislators granted very few charters and only after long, hard debate. Legislators usually denied charters to would-be incorporators when communities opposed the prospective business project.

"People did not want business owners hidden behind legal shields but in clear sight. That is what they got. As the Pennsylvania Legislature stated in 1834, '*A corporation in law is just what the incorporating act makes it.* It is the creature of the law and may be molded to any shape or for any purpose that the Legislature may deem most conducive for the general good.'

"During the late nineteenth century, however, corporations subverted state governments, and took over our power to put charters of incorporation to the uses originally intended. Under pressure from industrialists and bankers, a handful of judges gave corporations more rights in property than human beings enjoyed in their persons.

"Corporations persuaded courts to assume that they competed on equal terms with neighborhood businesses or individuals. Judges redefined the common good to mean maximum corporate production and profit.

"Corporations were abusing their charters to become conglomerates and trusts. They were converting the nation's treasures into private fortunes, creating factory systems and company towns. Political power began flowing to absentee owners intent upon dominating people and nature.

"Following the Civil War and well into the twentieth century, appointed judges gave privilege after privilege to corporations. They freely reinterpreted the U.S. Constitution and transformed common law doctrines.

"Judges gave certain corporations the power of eminent domain. They eliminated jury trials to determine whether corporations caused harm and to assess damages.

"Another blow to citizen constitutional authority came in 1886. The Supreme Court ruled in *Santa Clara County vs. Southern Pacific Railroad* that a private corporation was a 'natural person' under the U.S. Constitution and thus sheltered by the Bill of Rights and the Fourteenth Amendment. The high court ruled that elected legislators, in enabling people to protect their communities and livelihoods from corporate domination, had been taking corporate property without due process.

"Emboldened, some judges went further, declaring unions were civil and criminal conspiracies and enjoining workers from striking. Governors and presidents backed these judges with police and armies.

"Judges had positioned the corporation to become 'America's representative social institution,' 'an institutional expression of our way of life.'

"Today, many U.S. corporations are transnational. Still, no matter how piratical they may be or how far they may roam, the corrupted charter and bastardized state corporation code remain the legal bases of their existence."

("Exercising Power Over Corporations Through State Charters," Richard L. Grossman and Frank T. Adams, in *The Case Against the Global Economy*)

Guilt a word reserved for ethnic jokes.

The life we've created cried out for sedation.

But this morning is different.

The Devil we wake up to see every day, gazing at us in the bathroom mirror, for the first time refuses to fade away.

Tired of the game he's been playing for thousands of years, he turns himself inside out.

He huffs and he puffs and he pulls the plug on our oil supply.

He pulls the plug on a leaking medical system and waves of diseases surge through our bodies.

He pulls the plug on heat and electricity, on convoys of trucks lumbering obedient as cattle toward supermarkets, on shipping lanes crowded with supertankers, on skies thick with jumbo jets.

Instantaneously, all becomes silent.

All becomes clear.

"Scientists used to regard differentiation as a one-way street, with a cell capable of only going from an embryonic state to a mature one. It is now known that this process can and does reverse itself. For example, in wound healing the cells at the wound site must return to the embryonic state in order to heal."

(*Electromagnetic Fields,* B. Blake Levitt)

But the question is, will healing be permitted to take place?

Because the same mechanism present during healing also occurs in cancerous cells.

Cancer the infantile.

Cancer the narcissistic oneirophant, dreaming of eternal life on its own terms, never connecting, never backing off, never exhaling.

Renewal and self-destruction differ only in their context.

Healing requires contact, openness.

Cancer simply takes over.

Out of nowhere an ice maiden appears, uncanny in her blue and white perfection.

A moment later, dozens more.

Ice maidens all in a row, their smiles breaking glass, turning mother's milk to crystal, freezing conversation in mid-sentence.

Ice maidens, row upon row, multiplying to the horizon.

"I love myself," the maidens croon, obsessed with the magic of their involution, creating more and more of themselves, until the universe bursts with their breathless beauty.

Ice maidens anticipating the latest scientific breakthroughs.

Cancer furnishing the template for endlessness, for the clones of biotechnology's wet dream, the new genetics growing like Topsy, like tumors, like death-in-life.

Heal me, Momma. Momma heal me.

Take me back to the good old days.

I think back to the way things used to be.

The sixties, the seventies, the eighties.

Years spent in avoidance.

Years spent toking up.

High as a kite, seemingly content to let my life slip by.

From where did that surrender come?

From my mother. From her inability to leave my father, to start a new life. From her powerlessness, her indecision.

Dear Evelyn, my heart goes out to you. How you must have suffered. In therapy I blamed you but I don't blame you now. You were bewildered, frightened, caught in a maelstrom.

My father played the Devil in our little circle. He cut off my mother's life force. He took center stage, banishing her—banishing all of us—to the sidelines. And I didn't have the will to do battle with him. Instead I got stoned.

In thrall to marijuana.

Blind to my personal history.

Not understanding how I was structured by the past, *which always remains the same.*

The past reproducing itself, never showing its face, never relaxing its grip.

Without awareness, the same personality persisting from day to day, month to month, year to year.

In thrall to marijuana I became a spectator, proud of my neutrality, convinced that the game taking place on the field below me was corrupt.

In thrall to marijuana, in love with sensual surfaces and the play of the mind, I wrote hundreds of thousands of words.

I created parallel worlds where, without my realizing it, the protagonists were always victims.

I lived alone, listening intently to the music of the spheres.

I became a Buddhist, which maybe gave me freedom from my projections but also encouraged me to flee from Earth's muddy entanglements.

Sky gods were my heroes.

But when I sat down to write, victimhood wriggled onto the page.

Year after year.

I had no children and wanted none.

I laughed at society's demands, always choosing the path of least resistance.

Bailing out.

Kissing the sky.

Then I began to work on myself, journeying with the mother plant, making new friends.

I stopped smoking weed.

I abandoned the little cubicle in which I'd lived for so many years.

I learned to stay present, no matter what.

Released from the tentacles of the past, I offer my services.

I look for others of like mind.

What else is there to do with the time we have left?

It's a challenge, though.

Because marketing also speaks to the heart.

Nortel ad, looking down at me from a light box in the Miami Airport, February, 2001—

"*What do you want the Internet to be?*"

Soulful face of musician Carlos Santana, and his answer, scrawled as if by hand:

"*A road to a world with no borders, no boundaries, no flags, no countries. Where the heart is the only passport you carry.*"

A noble sentiment. How many of us haven't desired an end to arbitrary national borders?

But watch out, Carlos. Something spooky could be virusing its way into that wish of yours.

Because what if your heart's being taken for a ride by forces it fails to comprehend?

What if the obsolescence of nation-states is a prelude to something stickier?

If that's not the case, why is corporate colonialism considered a done deal, an irresistible tide?

Why does globalization mean the universal export of only American culture?

And creative marketing, dear reader—to what end?

"With huge expenditures on marketing, one-sixth of the gross domestic product, people pay for the privilege of being subjected to manipulation of their attitudes and behavior.

"The more 'free and popular' a government, the more it becomes necessary to rely on control of opinion to ensure submission to the rulers." (Noam Chomsky)

Polling specialists and public relations gurus fabricate the image and substance of political figures.

Slogans for packaging these figures and their programs are what the public gets to "decide" on.

The language used always turned inside-out.

If the public opposes dismantling the health system in order to "preserve, protect and strengthen" it for "the next generation," dismantling it is packaged as "a solution that preserves and protects the health system for the next generation."

Actual or hidden reality the opposite of public image.

The same reversal holds true for terms like *freedom, patriotism, reform, open market, rational,* and *individual.*

Democracy, for example, actually means top-down control to protect the opulent against the majority.

And *progress* results in greater and greater dependence, vulnerability.

"Capitalism wears the stage name *market economy,* imperialism is called *globalization,* opportunism is called *pragmatism,* poor people are called *low-income people*, the right of bosses to lay off workers with neither severance nor explanation is called *a flexible labor market*, thieves belonging to good families are called *kleptomaniacs*.

"In 1995, when France set off nuclear tests in the South Pacific, the French ambassador to New Zealand declared, 'I don't like that word *bomb*. They aren't bombs. They're exploding artifacts.'" (Eduardo Galeano)

In fact, you could qualify or put in quotation marks just about any phrase used to sell you something—*affordable luxury, natural ingredients, coastal evacuation route.*

All the above tasted within the larger context of your life, dear reader—

The context of *work*. (Another term with an altered meaning.)

By the early twentieth century, new forms of authoritarian rule had been institutionalized, including "the legitimation of wage labor, which was considered hardly better than slavery in mainstream America through much of the nineteenth century." (Noam Chomsky)

You probably didn't know that, because in a *free society* there's no history besides approved history.

In a *free society* the instruments of coercion are internalized.

Visitors to a country such as Colombia are shocked by the naked display of power—submachine-gun-toting guards stand in front of every bank.

Visitors to Myanmar, Guatemala, Nigeria, are dismayed by brazen monopoly control over mass media.

They congratulate themselves on living in *the free world.*

They don't realize that in Europe and the United States similar results are achieved by more civilized means.

Life's much better in Cleveland than in Lagos, certainly.

But does that mean Clevelanders are free?

"Communications manipulated by a handful of giants can be just as totalitarian as communications monopolized by the state. We are all obliged to accept freedom of expression as freedom of business." (Eduardo Galeano)

Look out, kid, they keep it all hid.

What can *public opinion polls* mean if we don't form our own opinions?

In 1949, doctrines crafted over previous decades were expressed in *Propoganda*, a manual of the public relations industry by one of its leading figures, Edward L. Bernays.

From *Profit Over People*—

"Bernays opens by observing that 'the conscious and intelligent manipulation of the organized habits and opinions of the masses is an important element in democratic society.' To carry out this essential task, 'the intelligent minorities must make use of propoganda continuously and systematically,' because they alone 'understand the mental processes and social patterns of the masses' and can 'pull the wires which control the public mind.'

"Therefore, our 'society has consented to permit free competition to be organized by leadership and propoganda.' Propoganda provides the leadership with a mechanism 'to mold the mind of the masses,' so that 'they will throw their newly gained strength in the desired direction.' The leadership can 'regiment the public mind every bit as much as an army regiments the bodies of its soldiers.' This process of 'engineering consent' is the very 'essence of the democratic process.'"

Obedient consumers forking over their life force for the benefit of people seriously drunk on their status as "winners."

And how do these winners maintain positions of power?

What atmosphere is encouraged at your basic successful transnational corporation?

Let's look at a leader in the field, General Electric.

GE's recent leap in share value resulted from adopting a super-aggressive management style.

"The idea of management by stress is to stretch production arrangements so as to eliminate any slack. Under this approach, all workers should be working their hardest, all the time, and the standard of what constitutes hard work should constantly be elevated.

"A series of internal GE documents reveals what pursuit of management by stress means in concrete terms. They show the company consciously seeking to maintain a high level of tension among workers, pressuring suppliers to move to low-wage countries by threatening to deny them GE contracts if they refuse; and operating management training schools that teach executives and mid-level managers how to implement management by stress and 'union avoidance' techniques.

"The jargon sprinkled throughout GE documents—'continuous improvement,' 'high performance,' 'developing and maintaining competitive advantage,' 'change acceleration process,' 'culture change,' 'change management,' 'human resources best practices,' 'productivity solutions'—conceals the human impacts of the global management by stress model. These include the psychological strain of living with constant fear of job loss, the physical risks of working on sped-up lines, and the community devastation resulting from GE shifting production around the world in search of ever lower cost wages."

("Global Management by Stress," Robert Weissman, in *Multinational Monitor*)

Speaking of sped-up lines, don't assume that the insistence on increased productivity is limited to the factory floor.

"The Information Revolution" of the 1990s was embraced as a way to wring more out of those who sit in front of computers.

In fact, in financial circles, prosperity itself is now conceived of as dependent upon a *yearly* increase in output from each hour's work.

The New York Times, September 3, 2001—

"Productivity is the principal contributor to economic growth. It determines whether corporate revenue is rising fast enough to increase wages and profits.

"The government's projection that it will accumulate a $3.4 trillion budget surplus between now and 2001 relies on a rate of productivity growth of at least two and a half percent. A more modest gain of two percent would be roughly $800 billion lower, according to the director of the Congressional Budget Office.

9.

Stay cool.

Don't panic.

The wireless revolution is here.

Wireless users now have access to powerful handheld devices that allow them to closely duplicate, if not directly replicate, the experience of being at home.

The advantage is that they can do it anyplace, at any time, without being attached to their hardwired connections.

Users can read any of thousands of magazines and newspapers on their PDAs (personal digital assistants).

If your first cell phone or laptop excited you, then read on.

Just the start of a revolution affecting virtually everyone.

Mobile/cell phone, laptop computer, PDA, pagers and two-way devices, wireless PDA modem, wireless laptop modem.

Question: Which handheld devices are critical?

Question: Do I need to replace my cell phone every three or four months?

Answer: While there is a seeming convergence among previously separate devices and applications, it does not appear that there will be a single device that satisfies the majority of consumer requirements.

Prospective buyers are encouraged to visit stores and see and touch these devices.

Cell-phone addict hunched over your device, with the apologetic or defiant demeanor of a nicotine freak—do you care to know the dangers in store for you?

Microwaves are aimed through your brain from the antenna of your little instrument.

No one can say for sure what will manifest ten or twenty years down the line.

Industry insists that what it makes is perfectly safe.

It releases favorable results of tests it has commissioned.

With so much riding on these results, what else do you expect?

But what about the stories of brain cancer already surfacing, a scant few years after the introduction of cell phones and other wireless devices?

What about the lawsuits settled out of court?

They include gag orders imposed as part of the settlement, so no unfavorable publicity can appear.

What about funds denied researchers, who have been almost completely shut out of investigating radio wave/microwave interaction with the human body?

Electromagnetic Fields, B. Blake Levitt—

"We see more and more towers with several dishes mounted on them blinking on the horizon . . . They perch atop our hospitals, municipal buildings, apartment houses, police and fire stations. They seem to pop up overnight on school property or appear in vacant fields near our homes. They dot the highways like bizarre outcroppings. We see single towers, small groups of varying heights and styles, and whole antenna farms.

"We simply don't know what a safe level of radio-frequency radiation is, yet we continue to increase our exposure to it every day.

"RF transmission signals are present in the environment all the time. Just turning off your radio or TV does not mean that the exposure disappears. If you get good radio and TV reception without a cable hookup, you live in a high-exposure environment."

Please don't nod out on me, dear reader.

The juicy stuff's coming right up.

"The power-density measurement is often linked to its ability to heat human tissue. RF/MW energy is absorbed by the human anatomy—described by the term specific absorption rate (SAR).

"One criticism of such a standard is that it allows for the power intensity to exceed that limit if it is for less than six minutes. But no one really checks the time period—and it is the higher intensities for short durations, which simulate pulsed exposures, that are of greatest concern. Anyone living near a cellular transmitter, for instance, would experience short, intense exposures all the time."

Does the foregoing apply to you?

Not if you're living in deep country, maybe.

All other readers, *caveat emptor.*

Do you see a parallel here between turning up the heat on human tissue and global warming?

Isn't the Devil's work the same in both instances?

What speeds up, heats up.

Smaller, faster, cheaper.

More crowded, more intense.

Cooked to a turn in short, intense exposures.

As in references to hellfire in the Holy Book.

To which, I remind you, eighty percent of your compatriots subscribe.

They're quite comfortable with the idea of getting scorched.

They even expect it.

"The Revelation of Jesus Christ which God gave unto him, to show unto his servants things which must shortly come to pass. For the time is at hand."

What hasn't occurred to them, apparently, is that the heating process already might be taking place.

It could be gradual and ongoing.

"We have not made much attempt to identify the resonant frequencies of other species, but there is the possibility that we are triggering critical parameters in some of them. For instance, frogs are disappearing all over the globe. Research in the 1920s discovered that frogs' eggs were affected by the 20 Hertz frequency. More recent research conducted in the 1970s . . . found that microwaves could alter the heart rhythm of frogs—including stopping it altogether—when the pulse was synchronized with the heartbeat. Numerous studies have found changes in the blood-brain barrier in test animals exposed to microwaves. Yet over one hundred thousand new cellular towers alone are planned in America—all broadcasting in the microwave frequencies." (B. Blake Levitt)

Planned as of 1995, that is.

Now spreading like wildfire.

Shall we continue?

Real information is interesting.

Partly because it brings up the question of why it's suppressed.

Because real information is always suppressed.

Or is "suppressed" too harsh a word?

How about ignored?

Conveniently overlooked?

Sarcastically dismissed?

"Whole communities and organizations can manifest group denial, which occurs when the subject under discussion is complex or has important implications for the status quo.

"And 'groupthink' can develop within an organization in which loyalty or the need to reach a consensus becomes more important than solving the problem at hand." (B. Blake Levitt)

For example, did you know the FDA has issued an advisory warning that hand-held cell phones should be used only when necessary and that conversations be kept brief?

Cell phones are not like conventional telephones, B. Blake informs us.

Children should not use them at all except in an emergency.

Cell phones can emit more radiation than the FDA allows for microwave ovens, yet they're currently exempt from FCC regulations.

Who's making the profit on these potential time bombs?

Why aren't they held responsible for their actions?

But I forgot—no one in particular is responsible.

Show me one corner of the corporate realm which doesn't sweep under the carpet any evidence of harmful activity—falsifying reports, firing whistle-blowers, developing camouflage technology as part of their game plan.

Caught red-handed, they'll reform to a minimal degree.

Then spend much more on advertising which trumpets to the world how pure they are.

The nature of the beast, you say.

Gee, maybe you're right.

Ms. Levitt cites numerous studies showing adverse health effects among workers in the electrical professions.

Elevated levels of leukemia, cancers of the stomach and intestines, lymphoma, abnormal development of fetuses, chromosomal breaks in blood lymphocytes, primary brain tumors, skin cancer, male breast cancer, Alzheimer's disease, amyotrophic lateral sclerosis.

Studies from the 1940s through the 1990s.

In Los Angeles, England, Canada, Sweden, Taiwan, New Zealand, France, Finland, New York City, the U.S. Navy.

Involving power-station operators, electricians and electrical engineers, aluminum processors, utility and telephone line workers and splicers, communications workers, radio operators, radio/TV repair workers, computer repair personnel, welders, flame cutters, cable joiners, sewing machine operators, and miners exposed to electrical distribution lines strung overhead in mine shafts.

"New studies come in every month," she writes. "There are currently hundreds being conducted in various countries. The question is, how many studies are enough?"

And we haven't even touched the topic of synthetic chemicals in the environment, in our blood.

Presumably you're already well-informed in that regard.

You know that twenty new chemicals enter the marketplace every week.

You know that eighty-three of the eighty-four synthetic chemicals in your blood have been there only since the 1950s.

You understand what effect these substances may be having on your health.

You understand how they may be combining with electromagnetic frequencies to short-circuit your system.

Far more bio-effects research exists for the above-cited power-line frequencies than for radio-frequency and microwave (RF/MW) bands, but what does exist is troubling.

"Many would say that the absence of RF/MW studies is not an accident, that important research has been systematically ignored, blocked, discredited . . . by those who stand to lose the most—the military and various segments of industry."

(Ah, the military—is there a connection between electromagnetic pulse or EMP weaponry and Gulf War Syndrome?)

RF/MW professions include broadcast engineers and employees of radio/TV transmission facilities, those working in multimedia environments, air traffic controllers, radar technicians, law enforcement officers who use radar guns, diathermy therapists and MRI technicians, airline personnel, and operators of RF heaters and sealers (shrink-wrappers).

Of course, those exposed to RF/MW bands also include people using cordless and cell phones, remote-control devices, walkie-talkies, microwave ovens.

And especially people living or working near cellular towers.

Here are a few of the surviving RF/MW studies—

"Stolodnik-Baranska reported in 1973 that human lymphocytes exposed to pulsed microwaves showed abnormalities directly related to the length of exposure.

"Henderson and Anderson reported in 1986 significantly elevated cancer rates in men and women living near broadcast towers in Honolulu.

"Lester and Moore reported in 1984 that neighborhoods exposed to radar waves from two airports in Wichita, Kansas, had a higher cancer incidence than nonexposed neighborhoods.

"Tynes reported in 1994 that women working as radio and telegraph operators for more than nine years (mostly aboard ships) were 80 percent more likely to develop breast cancer than nonexposed women."

And from among hundreds of animal studies dating back to the 1920s, we'll quote three—

"Guy reported in 1985 that several generations of rats exposed to pulsed microwaves in ranges that simulated the levels allowed by current standards for humans had increases in adrenal medulla tumors, malignant endocrine and ectocrine tumors, and increases in carcinomas and sarcomas.

"Salford and Persson reported in 1992 that increases in the permeability of the blood-brain barrier of rats could be effected at extremely low levels of microwave radiation of around 915 megahertz (around the frequencies used by cellular phones and cellular-phone towers).

"Sarkar reported in 1994 that the DNA of brain and testicular tissue in mice showed rearrangement following microwave exposure at 2.45 gigahertz at intensity levels currently considered safe." (B. Blake Levitt)

Currently considered safe.

Given the track record of the nuclear industry, of drug companies, tobacco companies, utility companies, paint manufacturers, pesticide manufacturers, petrochemical companies, the auto industry, junk-food producers, et cetera ad infinitum, why should we trust the telecommunications giants?

For example, electrical and mechanical objects now come equipped with remote control.

Nothing else available—whether TVs, cars, or appliances.

Remote-control devices emitting microwave radiation on which, remember, minimal testing has been done.

We'll work that out further down the line.

Meanwhile let's rake in the bucks.

Come to think of it, maybe such an attitude isn't reprehensible.

Maybe the transnationals secretly accept what the ancient Mayan calendar tells us—one more decade and we'll all be desaparecidos.

When the paradigm shift hits in the year 2012, brain cancer rates may just be starting their climb, but who will be around to notice?

In fact, who's around now?

Maybe memory loss itself *is* the paradigm shift.

Maybe it's already happened and we don't know it.

We've heard about the link between synthetic chemicals and the drop in sperm counts, the rise in hormone-related cancers.

Are we also seeing effects of an altered electromagnetic environment come to fruition?

Some new diseases, as well as dramatic increases in existing ones—

Learning disabilities and developmental defects in children, immune system disorders, chronic fatigue syndrome, Parkinson's disease, Hodgkin's disease.

And AIDS.

"HIV seemed to come out of nowhere," B. Blake writes.

"Researchers were able to create a mutation in the virus, which then caused the fatal syndrome. Their conclusion was interesting— that a subtle mutation could alter a minimally pathogenic virus into a deadly one capable of infecting and collapsing the immune system. EMFs are known to cause genetic mutations. Is there a link? Are those who develop AIDS already in a state of immune suppression when they become infected with HIV? It would appear so, because repeated exposures are often necessary for transmission of the virus. And once HIV has taken hold, chronic exposure to EMFs may play a significant role in the suppression of the immune system, thereby tilting the balance from a person being HIV-positive to developing full-blown AIDS."

And Alzheimer's.

"Just ten years ago [that is, 1985], this was considered an obscure and rare condition, but today it is the nation's fourth leading cause of death.

"Learning and memory are associated with a number of changes in the flow of potassium ions through cellular channels. Could an EMF resonance factor be involved with potassium ions? Melatonin is also known to be suppressed in those with Alzheimer's, and EMFs have been shown to lower melatonin in some studies. There is also some indication that microwave frequencies are particularly suspect. Repeated low-level nonthermal exposures to the eyes produced clinical Alzheimer's in test animals."

Diabolique

And then there's cancer.

Incidence of brain tumors risen threefold since the 1960s.

Prior to 1955, melanoma was quite rare, but from 1975 to 1992, cases in the United States alone tripled.

From 1973 to 1988, the breast cancer rate rose twenty-six percent.

"The incidence of all cancers has steadily risen in the United States since the turn of the century, even when smoking and the growth of the population are factored in. The prevalence of petrochemicals throughout the globe is probably a factor, and so is the steady increase in the use of artificially produced EMFs.

"Compared with what we know from fossilized remains of Stone Age civilizations, the occurrence of breast cancer in women is estimated to be one hundred times greater. Other studies have found that incidences of brain cancers and cancers of the endocrine system, of the blood and the skin have risen sharply since the turn of the century, in some cases spiking three hundred percent within the last two decades.

"Clearly something is turning our genetic apparatus on and off at cross-purposes with its normal sequence, activating the wrong things while suppressing the controls."

Turning on and off at cross-purposes.
Activating the wrong things.
Suppressing the controls.

The American Century tricking vegetable gardens into rows of identical concepts, pasture-ranging cows into cement-filled machines, galloping horses into upholstered steel boxes, houses built of local materials into universal concrete abstractions.

Tricking picnics on the grass into stand-up snacks inside a 7-11.

Tricking a rifle in our hands into bombs activated from the greatest possible distance.

Tricking the curiosity of little boys into lethal experiments on unsuspecting "volunteers."

At the very least, why can't we admit we don't know what we're doing?

Now for the nitty-gritty.

The incidence of Alzheimer's in the past ten years has sky-rocketed.

You remember that, don't you?

You also remember various reasons for this phenomenon were put forward.

But what about the larger picture?

Not how, but why?

Why is the American brain so swiftly self-destructing?

In a flash it's full of plaque and tangles.

Its tissues come to resemble long strands of gray knotted rubber.

And the possessor doesn't even get the chance to reflect, much less repent.

In 1995, my father died of Alzheimer's.

I'll spare you the details, dear reader.

Except to say that in the space of a few months an overbearing tyrant became an infant, grinning, helpless, radiating idiot wonder.

Someone toward whom it was suddenly impossible to feel anger.

Born again, my father shed his personality, and what else is there to hold responsible for someone's acts?

He could have done anything in his life and, with this turn of events, escaped his day of reckoning.

Like Ronald Reagan, for instance, he could have allowed atrocities to be committed in Central America, Grenada, Iran.

Like Ronald Reagan, he could have wrapped himself in the American flag while bleeding its poor.

Like Ronald Reagan, he could've cracked jokes about trees as the major source of air pollution.

Your father, my father, Ron Reagan's father.

The Devil in blue jeans and cowboy boots.

The Devil peeking out from under his shock of unruly hair with an aw-shucks grin, charming the pants off of anyone he meets.

The Devil not even knowing he's the Devil.

Ah, but there's nothing you can do, it's too late, he's lost his marbles.

He's become one of God's innocents, drooling into his porridge.

And where once you raged, now your heart aches with sadness.

The opportunity for connection gone, the chance to communicate lost.

Yes, Dad, I loved you in spite of everything.

Because at the level of source you remained sweet and clear—no matter who you were, no matter what you did.

That's the way of the world.

Poor brain, unmoored by gale-force winds of an ego-driven culture.

And before you know it, the Devil's lost his memory.

Just as, in order to keep functioning, America forgets its crimes.

Crimes without which it could not remain triumphant.

Triumphant over enemies it alone has created.

Self-created like the enemies who tormented my father.

(*Around and around it goes*
Where it stops nobody knows)

Alzheimer's culture, culture of the vacant stare, culture of sheer disconnect.

The survival of global capitalism depends on constant growth.

Excitedly my father pointed out the window of his hospital room.

"Tree!" he shouted. "Grows big a million!"

With each passing decade, America becomes more infantile.

And the noise of Collosus is deafening.

Oil rigs slam into the Earth's heart, louder and louder.

No one hears.

No one notices.

No one remembers.

10.

Try to keep the above in mind while we take a brief look at so-called current events.

Though we know they never really occur in the present but always in the past.

Though we feel the toxic breeze of the end times on our faces.

And the call of the last unmodified bird grates on our doctored nerves.

Still, it seems like just yesterday that the 2000 U.S. presidential election was stolen.

Pay no mind to the relative merits of the men running for office.

What matters is the ruthlessness with which the issue was decided.

What matters is the co-optation of the law by interested parties.

This is what is meant by "the rule of law."

This is how the State operates.

This is its nature, its essence.

It exists to be used by those who hold the power.

Remember the U.S. Supreme Court's blatant rupture of the vote count in Florida?

Remember its follow-up, full of obfuscation, in which the country was presented with a fait accompli?

And finally, do you remember the swiftness with which an interloper was handed the presidency with all the trappings of legitimacy?

Normal life goes on.

The supposed wound to the nation's psyche healed in record time.

In a matter of days all was forgotten.

"In effect, each one of us carries within himself, internalized like the believer's faith, the certitude that society exists for the State." (Pierre Clastres)

The New York Times, Austin, Texas, December 19, 2000—
"With natural gas prices at an all-time high and Americans facing power shortages in some states, President-elect Bush's plans for an energy policy have started to receive close scrutiny.

"His most controversial idea during the campaign—opening Alaskan wilderness to drilling—has enraged environmental advocates. And debate over the drilling has overshadowed other ideas Mr. Bush is considering that could have much wider impacts on energy supplies and the environment.

"Industry officials said they also expected him to take steps to rejuvenate coal and nuclear power while considering ways to curb the Environmental Protection Agency and other agencies, making it easier for energy companies to build power plants, refineries, natural gas pipelines and transmission lines.

"Mr. Bush did not talk about specific pieces of energy legislation. But once in office, Ari Fleischer, the Bush transition spokesman said, he plans to direct the Energy Department to review federal lands currently off-limits to drilling.

"Robert J. Allison Jr., chairman and chief executive of the Anadarko Petroleum Corporation in Houston, said, 'A lot of federal lands are off-limits in a way that doesn't make sense and that can be developed in an environmentally friendly way.'

"'The most important thing,' Mr. Allison said, 'is that we have access to places to drill.'"

Notice how language is used here, dear reader.
Why should protected lands be despoiled for at most six years worth of energy?

Do you trust the phrase "environmentally friendly"?

Is there any connection between drilling for natural gas and addressing the problem of power shortages?

How easy is it for you to spot the greed peeking out of every paragraph?

Understand that Mr. Bush, his cronies, and many of his appointees are the oil industry.

Realize that nowhere above is development of alternative energy sources mentioned.

Consider that the energy crisis referred to might be minor, temporary, or even intentional.

Glance at the calendar as you read this.

What's today's date?

How much of the above has already come to pass?

What other areas of potential profit have been approached in similar fashion?

(*The New York Times*, Washington, D.C., May 1, 2001—

"Vice President Dick Cheney said today that oil, coal and natural gas would remain the United States' primary energy resources for 'years down the road' and that the Bush administration's energy strategy would aim mainly to increase supply of fossil fuels, rather than limit demand.

"Mr. Cheney dismissed as 1970s-era thinking the notion that 'we could simply conserve or ration our way out' of what he called an energy crisis.

"The only solution, he said, is a government-backed push to find new domestic resources of oil and gas, including in protected areas of the Arctic National Wildlife Refuge, and an all-out drive to build power plants—a need that he says will require one new electricity-generating plant a week for twenty years.

"He estimated that the country needed 38,000 miles of new pipelines to carry natural gas, covering the distance of Maine to California more than twelve times over."

Gosh, that didn't take long at all.

Some people must be in an awful hurry.)

Speaking of wildlife refuges—

Corcovado National Park, Costa Rica, February, 2001.

Early morning walk through primary rainforest.

Raucous scarlet macaws sail through the treetops of this jungle canopy.

"What's that smell?" I ask my guide. Sweet, musty.

"Monkey piss," she whispers. "It means they're nearby."

I look up to see a band of chocolate-brown spider monkeys swinging from limb to limb.

High above my head, one pauses to stare at me.

Toucans, doves, dozens of other birds I can't identify, their calls sliding through the green.

Red passionflower blooming in the shadows, will the emerald hummingbird beside me pollinate you?

A luminous blue morpho butterfly floats and twists along the path in front of us.

During our hour-long walk, a half-dozen other species appear.

And as we're leaving, heard but not seen, the deafening call and response of a large troop of howler monkeys.

Bellowing in unison somewhere in the forest.

Pausing.

Beginning again from farther away.

Drifting through time.

And the trees, the vines, the shrubs and snakes and insects—I can't begin to name them.

Yes, dear reader, I've entered this place an almost complete illiterate, barely able to make out a few words of its rich text.

My heart burns as I compare the rainforest around me to what I saw the day before from the taxi which was taking me to the nearest town, an hour's boat ride away from here—

Mile after mile of banana and palm oil plantations.

Now and then the oppressive sameness parted to reveal a vista of sagging shacks lined up in the naked sun.

The workers' quarters.
Called home by some.

Moon Handbooks: Costa Rica, Christopher P. Baker—

"In the time it takes you to read this page, some thirty-two hectares of the world's tropical rainforests will be destroyed. The statistics defy comprehension. One hundred years ago, rainforests covered two billion hectares, fourteen percent of the Earth's land surface. Now only half remains, and the rate of destruction is increasing: an area larger than the state of Florida is lost every year. If the destruction continues apace, the world's rainforests will vanish within forty years.

"Despite Costa Rica's achievements in conservation, deforestation continues at an alarming rate.

"The humid *llanura* is the biggest piece of primeval rainforest left on the Caribbean rim, a tiny enclave of the original carpet that once covered most of lowland Central America. Very wet and isolated, these mist-enshrouded waves of green have been relatively untouched by man until recently. Today, the lowlands resound with the carnivorous buzz of chain saws; in the 'dry' season, in isolated patches, they are on fire.

"Cattle ranching has been particularly wasteful. Large tracts of virgin forest were felled in the 1960s to make way for cattle, stimulated by millions of dollars of loans provided by U.S. banks and businesses promoting the beef industry to feed the North American market.

"Many animal and plant species can survive only in large areas of wilderness. Most rainforest species are so highly specialized that they are quickly driven to extinction by the disturbance of their forest homes.

"Once the rainforests have been felled, they are gone forever. Despite their abundant fecundity, the soils on which they grow are generally very poor, thin and acidic.

"When humans cut the forest down, the organic-poor soils are exposed to the elements and are rapidly washed away by the intense rains, and the ground is baked by the blazing sun to leave an infertile wasteland."

Diabolique

Global warming, rainforests on fire, oil rigs flaring in the night.
Wherever fortunes are made the mansions of the rich get bigger and brighter.
Empty ballrooms illuminated for show, banks of windows ablaze.
While down in the slums, searchlights finger more and more people.
And on the avenues and freeways it's always high noon.
American paranoia keeping the planet well-lit.
No wonder the Devil dresses in red.
He turns up the temperature to increase the speed.
Pedal to the metal.
Smaller, faster, cheaper.

American free markets
American technologies
American styles
American products
American values
American norms
American fast food
Hollywood movies
Being globalized on Monday
American free markets
American technologies
American styles
American products
American values
American norms
American fast food
Hollywood movies
Being globalized on Tuesday
American free markets
American technologies

American styles
American products
American values
American norms
American fast food
Hollywood movies
Being globalized on Wednesday
American free markets
American technologies
American styles
American products
American values
American norms
American fast food
Hollywood movies
Being globalized on Thursday
American free markets
American technologies
American styles
American products
American values
American norms
American fast food
Hollywood movies
Being globalized on Friday
American free markets
American technologies
American styles
American products
American values
American norms
American fast food
Hollywood movies
Being globalized on Saturday
But on Sunday America rests.
On Sunday the primal forests reappear

Filled with vanished plants and animals.
On Sunday lakes sparkle in the sunlight
Filled with the fish which were absent.
On Sunday the rivers run clean
As they pass self-sufficient villages and towns
Where everyone lives out the dream of their origins.
Dressed in traditional costumes
Arms linked in community
They spill out into the squares and parks
Singing the old songs.
(Don't worry, this is just a little fairy tale.
Something to pass the time.
Your stocks are still snug in their portfolios.
Your car alarm still functions.
As you stumble into the bathroom on Monday morning, your medicine chest still awaits you.
You step into the kitchen and your container of antibiotic milk stands guard.
Rest assured, America still carries the day—your milk tastes exactly the same on every planet in the Milky Way.)

Why does the United States have the world's highest incidence of osteoporosis?
Why does China, where dairy products are rarely consumed, have a far lower incidence?
"According to a Harvard Nurses' Health Study which followed 77,761 women aged thirty-four to fifty-nine for twelve years, those getting substantial calcium from milk experienced more fractures than those drinking little or no milk.
"A 1994 study of the elderly in Sydney, Australia—those with the highest dairy consumption had double the risk of hip fracture compared to those with the lowest consumption."
(The Physicians' Committee for Responsible Medicine—www.pcrm.org)
Milk as a source of usable calcium is dairy industry propaganda.

Better to ask what cow's milk ever replaced in the human diet in the first place.

Before the domestication of cows, our forebears evolved normal skeletons.

Clearly, their food provided them with the necessary calcium.

"No signs of rickets may be detected on High Period Greek and Egyptian bones.

"Doctors in the days of Hippocrates never reported any cases of narrow pelvises.

"Rickets only became common under the new scenario in Europe after the Middle Ages."

(*Diseases at the Dawn of Western Civilization,* Mirko D. Grmek.)

Milk-drinking gluts the body with phosphorus, which prevents enteric absorption of calcium.

The bottle-fed child tends to have low blood calcium.

The liver and kidneys of a bottle-fed child are thirty percent larger than those of a breast-fed child.

The milk drinker's body is forced to take calcium from bones in order to achieve a proper calcium/phosphorous ratio.

Osteoporosis being the end result.

And pasteurization is even worse.

Pasteurization alters bonds holding minerals together, further preventing calcium from being utilized.

The milk drinker's body must use its own minerals from an already depleted supply to handle the excess acids introduced into it.

Depletion of minerals in the milk drinker's body mimicking depletion in the farmer's soil.

Calves fed on pasteurized cow's milk will die in three to four months.

We kings of creation dream up a more roundabout process.

Coating our bowels with dairy mucus which suppresses immune response.

Overdosing on animal protein which lodges in the intestines, kidneys, and liver, and saturates our blood with ammonia.

Becoming exhausted and disease-prone as we "age."

Assuming that such deterioration is natural.

Turning to pharmaceuticals for help.

Not wondering how insurance companies determine when we should retire from work.

Not noticing that the functioning of the economy depends on moving us right along.

Not realizing that the economy would falter if older people remained vigorous.

As gullible as chickens, we peck at what's put before us.

As trusting as cows, we head straight for the exit.

Food's not something simply to push into the mouth, chew, and swallow.

Sawdust and perfume could be used for that.

In fact, they already are.

Ask those assembly-line cows and chickens about the concoctions they're fed.

Ask the newborn calves shut up in stalls so tiny they can hardly move.

Slaughtered after four months of darkness to produce the milky flesh gourmands prize.

As soft and white as death.

Beyond Beef, Jeremy Rifkin—

"Modern meat is a testimonial to the utilitarian ethos. The spirit of the animal is ruthlessly repressed and deadened shortly after birth.

"To ease their consciences, modern men and women have erected a series of barriers designed to distance themselves as much as possible from the animals they eat. By removing themselves from an intimate relationship with their prey, they have been able to suppress deep-seated emotional connections and the fear, shame, disgust, and regret that often accompany killing a fellow creature.

"Enlightenment thinkers objectified nature, transforming it into a resource and commodity, endowing it with machinelike attributes in order to justify ruthless technological manipulation and commercial expropriation. The beef-eating cultures have further separated themselves from the animals they eat by shifting blame for their deaths, concealing the act of slaughter, misrepresenting the process of dismemberment, and disguising the identity of the animal during food preparation."

The Devil was visualized by the early Church with cloven hooves, horns, and a tail.
Animal turned inside out, from fellow creature to force of evil.
But we're smarter than that now.
We see the real connection between cattle and evil.

"The modern cattle complex represents a new kind of malevolent force in the world.
"Cold evil is evil inflicted from a distance; evil concealed by layer upon layer of technological and institutional garb . . . To suggest that a person is committing an evil act by growing feed for cattle or consuming a hamburger might appear strange, even ludicrous.
"Chances are that the supermarket manager who stocks the grain-fed beef will never personally experience the anguish of those millions of families thrown off their land so that it can be used to grow livestock feed for export. Teenagers gobbling down cheeseburgers at a fast-food restaurant will likely be unaware that a wide swath of tropical rainforest had to be felled and burned to bring them their meal. Consumers buying prepackaged cuts of steak will never know the pain and discomfort experienced by animals in high-tech automated feedlots.
"The story of humanity's long relationship to cattle is the story of our changing relationship to our own generativeness. The bull and the cow, ancient icons of our own virility and fertility, have been desacralized and denatured, stripped of their aliveness and turned into machines of production. They have been robbed of their being, deconstructed into sheer matter for manipulation, and made into things."

America, we still love you but you're full of shit.

Your only hope a major detox.

A national enema, a transnational colonic!

America, go on a vision quest.

Draw a circle around yourself in the wilderness and stay there for three days—seven days—twenty-one days.

Without food or water.

Completely silent and alone, humbly offering up your senses to the spirit surrounding you.

With purity of purpose, with humility and grace.

Surrender all pretense, all excuses and explanations.

Blow the poisons out of your gut.

Release the junk clogging your mind.

America, life is not property.

Break the globalization trance.

Abandon your cockeyed, reductive vision.

It's only resulted in ignorance, superstition, plague.

Only resulted in your essence owned by corporations.

Only resulted in you Americanizing the planet, making it over in your image as if you were God.

America, heal yourself.

Pull the plug on your addictions.

Open your eyes to the consequences of your actions.

Wash your hands of the blood which stains them.

Before your bloated ego brings the heavens crashing down around you.

If the opportunity for recovery even still exists.

Because, raving in darkness, you've sailed past the point of no return many times.

Without love your soul appears deformed.

Rigidity and fixation triumph.

(Before the end times hit, when traveling through airports or sitting in public places, I would play a little game.

I would force my gaze away from the TV monitors which were everywhere, spewing images of the distraction culture in all directions.

Then I scrutinized adult empire builders in the prime of life as they walked past me—the expressions in their eyes and on their faces, the condition of their bodies, the way they held themselves.

And then I visualized these people as young children.

I would see them the way they once were—innocent, pliable, clear.

Till I couldn't stand it anymore.)

11.

So what to do?

A tricky question.

Unless, dear reader, you're convinced the lights are still on, the banks and cafés are still open, the season tickets are still being printed.

Unless you believe Empire's still alive.

Because if you do, the answer's obvious—

Don't be discouraged by long odds.

Each moment exists only to break those odds.

You're immersed in a psychological continuum which, no matter how intense, can be ruptured more easily than you imagine.

Consensus reality is insubstantial.

It's made of nothing but images and beliefs.

The instant you change them, they vanish.

The instant you change them, a new world appears.

This demonic realm is a con game, arbitrary and vulnerable.

Remember biology's open secret—learning can be transmitted from one member of a species to another without direct communication or even any contact.

All it takes is intention.

Understand the power of that intention.

Embrace the magic of not knowing.

Study the concepts of critical mass, the tipping point, and singularity.

Refuse to give in to the done deal—it's bogus.

Laugh at anyone who tells you otherwise—they'll always say it's too late.

Global corporate media pushes the idea that there's no alternative.

But human values can change. They're not natural laws.

We can create a sustainable, dignified world.

How do mass movements begin?

Look to the farmers in India, poor peasants who organized against the terminator seed foisted on them by Monsanto and—against all odds—kicked the giant out.

Look to the Grameen Bank in Bangladesh—lending institution as social movement.

Look to the European campaign against genetically modified organisms.

Look to the American abolitionists, the labor movement, the consumer rights movement, feminism.

All began with a handful of people.

So too, you who are going to dismantle the demon.

Stop up your ears to global capital's siren song.

Corporations are confections.

Rewrite state charters, putting corporate control back in the hands of real people.

Erase the vision which has trashed this planet.

Refuse a techno-eugenic future.

Abandon the petrochemical nightmare in whatever way you can.

Learn from psychoactive plant substances, they are your oldest teachers.

Become ecologically literate—the only waste generated on this planet is by us.

Teach your children biodiversity.

End your reliance on pharmaceuticals.

Stop filling your face with dead food.

Reject the cattle culture and its myriad depredations.

Re-enter the garden of no work which is your birthright.

Before you know it, thousands will morph into millions.

All it takes is determination.

All you need is your intention.

So what to do?

A tricky question, here in my icy cabin in the sand, lit by the flares of oil rigs in the distance.

What's being sucked up out of the ground?

Petroleum or human blood?

Motor fuel or life essence?

Then I realize that it makes no difference.

Because, either way, my heart connects to the Goddess.

She alone will ride out this madness.

She alone will prevail.

My only responsibility is to her.

My only agenda, release from ego's stranglehold.

Because—for me at least—it's a bit late for provisional measures.

The year 2012 has come and gone.

The lights are out, the houses are cold, the shops are all rusted shut.

The big eighteen-wheelers lie belly-up by the side of the road.

Military bases around the world stand vacant.

Except for the oil machinery still pounding into the Earth, the show is over.

Disoriented masses of famished people pour into the streets.

Even the clones in their warehouses are hungry.

Under the circumstances, I feel justified in abandoning the dream of amelioration.

I burn my collection of proactive bumper stickers.

I bury my voter registration card for future generations to puzzle over.

No more writing eloquent letters to opaque congresspersons.

No more scouring sorrowful newspapers.

Their darkness comes off on my hands.

It lodges in my eyes.

No more rage.

Rage hurts no one but me.

No more enemies.

Their solidity is my creation.

TV not my enemy.
Petrochemicals not my enemy.
Pharmaceuticals not my enemy.
Capitalism not my enemy.
Globalization not my enemy.
America not my enemy.

Because I become the Devil when I lose myself in hatred.
I become the motherfucker when I blame and accuse.
Consensus reality—the only way to fight it is to release it.
The only freedom is freedom from my own fixations.

database

Freedom is imbecility.

But what about you—beautiful stranger, love of my life, mirage of completion?
Will we get another chance?
No sooner do I think of you than you appear naked at my cabin door under a lime and magenta sky, your head shaved, your eyes dazed, the Universal Price Code stamped on your forehead.
Your arms and legs are covered with sores.
You're no more than a walking skeleton.
Shivering from the cold, you ask for me to take you in.
And of course I do.
As long as you promise to hold onto nothing.
As long as you join me in a life without history, without expectations.
We get up in the morning, our minds clear and awake.
While scavenging for food we remain present.
While eating we remain present.
While making love we remain present.
While doing nothing we remain present.
We remain present while dumping our parade of heavy memories.
Memories which seem to take forever to dissipate but what's the rush, my darling?

Where else is there to go?

We remain present while surrendering to the Goddess.

While polishing the necklace of skulls she wears, we place our-selves in her care.

Mountains crumble, cities vanish, rivers of humanity drown in their own tears.

The entire universe a melee of shooting stars and blazing wis-dom fire.

The Goddess always smiling.

(As the ancient texts averred.)

Emptiness, my great friend.

As soon as appearance manifests, in that very moment is empti-ness.

Great covenant, untainted by signs of rejecting and accepting.

Great pervasiveness, knots of hope and fear released.

Beyond internal and external, beyond conception, transparent, unobstructed space.

Without difficulty and effort I take refuge.

Sources

(in order of appearance in text)

Chomsky, Noam. *Profit Over People: Neoliberalism and Global Order.* New York: Seven Stories Press, 1999.

Shiva, Vandana. "Blind Technology: Genetic Engineering of Mustard for Blindness Prevention." *Bija Newsletter* (New Delhi, India), January 2001.

Korten, David C. *When Corporations Rule the World.* West Hartford, CT: Kumarian Press, 1995.

Galeano, Eduardo. *Upside Down: A Primer for the Looking-Glass World.* New York: Henry Holt, 2000.

Bird, Christopher, and Peter Tompkins. *Secrets of the Soil: New Solutions for Restoring Our Planet.* Anchorage, AL: Earthpulse Press, 1998.

Elgin, Duane. *Promise Ahead: Towards a Way of Life That Transforms the Present and Safeguards the Future.* New York: HarperCollins, 2001.

Robbins, John. *Diet for a New America.* Walpole, NH: Stillpoint Press, 1987.

Young, Robert O., and Shelley Redford Young. *Sick and Tired?: Reclaim Your Inner Terrain.* Pleasant Grove, UT: Woodland Publishing, 1999.

Rinpoche, Thrangu. "Pointing Out the Dharmakaya." *Shenpen Ösel* 4, No. 3, December 2000.

Baudrillard, Jean. *The Vital Illusion.* Edited by Julia Witwer. New York: Columbia University Press, 2000.

Rifkin, Jeremy. *The Biotech Century.* New York: Jeremy P. Tarcher/Putnam, 1998.

Ho, Mae-Wan. "The Human Genome Sellout." *Third World Resurgence* (Penang, Malaysia), November/December 2000.

Mooney, Pat Roy. "The ETC Century: Erosion, Technological Transformation and Corporate Concentration in the 21st Century." *Development Dialogue* 1–2 (Uppsala, Sweden), 1999.

Clastres, Pierre. *Archeology of Violence.* Translated by Jeanine Herman. New York: Semiotext(e), 1994.

Clastres, Pierre. *Society Against the State.* Translated by Robert Hurley with Abe Stein. New York: Zone Books, 1987.

DeKorne, Jim. *Psychedelic Shamanism.* Port Townsend, WA: Breakout Productions, 1994.

Virilio, Paul. *The Information Bomb.* Translated by Chris Turner. New York: Verso Books, 2000.

Shiva, Vandana. *Monocultures of the Mind: Perspectives on Biodiversity and Biotechnology.* London: Zed Books, 1993.

Norberg-Hodge, Helena. "The Pressure to Modernize and Globalize." In *The Case Against the Global Economy: And for a Turn Toward the Local,* edited by Jerry Mander and Edward Goldsmith. San Francisco: Sierra Club Books, 1996.

Mander, Jerry. "The Rules of Corporate Behavior." In *The Case Against the Global Economy: And for a Turn Toward the Local,* ibid.

Grossman, Richard L., and Frank T. Adams. "Exercising Power Over Corporations Through State Charters." In *The Case Against the Global Economy: And for a Turn Toward the Local,* ibid.

Levitt, B. Blake. *Electromagnetic Fields: A Consumer's Guide to the Issues and How to Protect Ourselves.* New York: Harcourt Brace, 1995.

Weissman, Robert. "Global Management by Stress." *Multinational Monitor* 22, No. 7 & 8, July/August 2001.

Uchitelle, Louis. "Notions of New Economy Hinge on Pace of Productivity Growth." *The New York Times,* 3 September 2001.

Oppel, Richard A. and Neela Banerjee. "The Forty-third President: The Power Industry." *The New York Times,* 19 December 2000.

Kahn, Joseph. "Cheney Promotes Increasing Supply as Energy Policy." *The New York Times,* 1 May 2001.

Baker, Christopher P. *Moon Handbooks: Costa Rica.* Emeryville, CA: Avalon Travel Publishing, 1999.

Rifkin, Jeremy. *Beyond Beef: The Rise and Fall of the Cattle Culture.* New York: Plume Books, 1993.

Acknowledgments

Thanks to Nick Dorsky for opening the gate, to Rudy Wurlitzer, Daniel Pinchbeck, and David Korten for generous suggestions, and to Sally Egbert for spontaneous presence.

To Joanna Yas, managing editor extraordinaire.

And to all those who are dismantling the demon:

"Although the challenges we face may seem to be evidence of humanity's failures, reaching this stage is actually an expression of our great success over the past thirty-five thousand years. The apparent crises we face are, in reality, part of our initiation into a new relationship with one another and the Earth." (Duane Elgin)